BEST WISHES, SISTER B

Fran Smith teaches GCSE English and English as a Foreign Language. Before becoming a teacher she worked for the Probation Service for ten years. Her first job after school was on the Buckinghamshire Advertiser, where, among other things, she wrote wedding reports and the People and Pets column. She lives in a village at the edge of the Fens.

BEST WISHES, SISTER B

FRAN SMITH

THREE HARES PUBLISHING

Published by Three Hares Publishing 2014

First published in Great Britain in 2014
www.threeharespublishing.com

Three Hares Publishing Ltd Reg. No 8531198
Registered address: Suite 201, Berkshire House,
39-51 High Street,
Ascot, Berkshire, SL5 7HY

ISBN 9781910153000

I blame Chris for this

Sisters Worldwide Writing Circle

Letters from sisters all over the world to sisters all over the world

Application

*Please give your name and say why you are interested
in joining the Sisters Worldwide Writing Circle. We will
do our best to find you a suitable correspondent.*

Name: Emelda Griggs (Member of the Order of St Hilda)

Hello Sisters,

*My calling brought me to the Peruvian Andes fourteen years ago to teach
and do research among remote communities. I am blessed to stay among
wonderfully welcoming people and I never lack company – but I am a
team of one. It is very rare to speak English and I haven't met a sister
for over a decade.*

*I am originally from Suffolk and the longer I am in the mountains,
the more I miss the Fens! If your organization could find me a correspondent in a quiet country convent, who could share with me the humble
details of the daily convent round, I feel certain her letters would sustain
me in a way that nothing else could.*

*I rely on handwritten letters carried long distances by mule train or
canoe, so my replies may be infrequent, but any letter I receive will be a
treasured and delightful reminder of home.*

*With love and blessings,
Emelda*

Please write to La Hermana Ingles, c/o Convent of Santo
Domingo, Santa Maria del las Rocas, Valdepenas, Peru

1

SISTERS WORLDWIDE

Dear Sister Emelda,

Fourteen years of bringing education and prayer to the remote parts of Peru is a wonderful achievement, especially since your Mother Abbess says you left Norwich with £12.60 and one small duffel bag. A solitary calling, especially one that takes you to such mountainous and dangerous places, is immensely inspiring. Our work here in Three Fens seems flat in every way by comparison, but you specified "humble details of the daily convent round" and those I can certainly provide, so here goes.

First an introduction: I am Boniface. I have several roles here at St Winifreda's: I am the qualified minibus driver; I teach English as a foreign language to visitors; I am this year's Sisters Worldwide correspondent for handwritten letters (as you see) and very soon I will be running our new Convent Shoppe. We carried out a 'skills audit' and, although I have absolutely no shop keeping experience, I was hopeless at handicrafts and cookery and only considered good for heavy work in the garden, so it was a process of elimination, really.

The Shoppe is one of the initiatives we have adopted since the arrival of our new Rev Mother, Elizabeth, in the New Year. What a firebrand! She came to us after a re-organisation of the diocese closed three small convents and is determined that St Winifreda's will "re-group, re-fund and re-vivify" – she's a great one for a slogan. We are well-advanced with our plans to convert to sustainable energy, become self-sufficient in fruit and vegetables and generate new income streams (as they call it – we went to a Fenbiz seminar) with guest rooms and a website. It's very exciting.

I am enclosing a pen and ink drawing of St Winifreda's. It's my own attempt, and a bit rough, but will have to do until Father Humbert's ganglion improves (he is our parish priest and a talented artist). Most of the buildings date from the 1780s, apart from the bell tower on the right, which is a 19th century addition. You can just see the Shoppe to the left, and if you look very carefully you can even see the telescope in the orchard.

Sisters Angelina and Merce are our oldest residents at over a hundred, and also our resident astronomers. Our youngest member is a novice, Hermione, in her twenties. We have a very active exchange programme and welcome sisters from orders all over the world, so we're very cosmopolitan. At present we have visitors from Columbia, Sri Lanka, Poland, Albania and Kenya, all bringing their various skills. We also have a retirement home for sisters from many different orders.

As you know, Emelda, sisters never really retire, so until ill health slows them down, most are active and fully involved with the life of the convent. I know them well because I do the driving when there is a visit to the doctor or outpatients; never a dull moment with a minibus-load of them, I can promise you.

I am writing this in the back room of the Shoppe. We all hope it will be a major fundraiser since major funds (and come to that even minor ones) are in short supply. Like you, we have a heavenly banker, so obviously we don't worry about such matters, but every now and then there is a little crisis and the buildings aren't getting any younger. As someone who has travelled the world on a budget of less than £13 you perhaps think us very faint of heart, but last year the damp invaded the dormitory wing so badly that six cells were only fit for growing mushrooms and the surveyor refused to go in without breathing apparatus and a hard hat, despite the fact that Sister Dymphna was still living there quite happily. She was shot at by Nazis, so a bit of fungus wasn't shifting her.

Anyway, we are squaring up to the challenges of shop keeping very boldly. I have studied Retail for Beginners and Customer Service 1, and Starting a Small Business (all free one day courses and a complimentary pen every time) thanks to the EU Fenbiz initiative.

We found an old doorbell and I have painted, though I say it myself, a very lovely open/closed sign. One of our neighbours donated a handsome till with a very satisfying *ching!* and once we have stocked our few shelves with homegrown produce all will be ready for the grand opening. A quick blessing tomorrow morning and at 8.30am sharp I turn the sign round and wait for the customers to surge in. There is already a sign in the lane: "St Winifreda's Convent Shoppe Opening SOON!" and tonight, just before prayers, I will paste "TODAY!" over "SOON!" Who could resist?

We have a rather small stock at present, mainly eggs, spring greens, broad beans and a few of last year's potatoes. We are not sure what our customers will demand, or indeed who they will be. That was the hardest part of the business plan, really, because we are not near a main road, so everyone except the nearby farmers and the people from the small business units up the lane have to make a special detour to get to us, and we're not sure they will. We'll just pray.

I was also not sure how to set our prices. The only way was to go undercover to Tesco and make a note of a few of theirs. This felt almost like industrial espionage and we had to offer it up in prayers to make sure it wasn't actually dishonest. But Hari Menon, our Fenbiz mentor, said, "Oh no Sister, don't worry, this is not snooping, this is merely good business practice." Hardly a day goes by, apparently without a Tesco man or an Aldi woman with a notebook sidling into his shops – he has three – but he never gives it a thought. "Ah, the challenge of competition, Sister, so very satisfying and exciting, you will see!"

So the plan is to sell homegrown vegetables and eggs and perhaps soon a few useful household things like soap or dusters. And between customers I imagine there will be plenty of time to write letters and even give a quick English lesson. I hope so because Sister Vlora has been stuck at pre-intermediate for far too long already.

Now I must go and collect the eggs – Carmella is too busy cutting spring greens and Joan of Ark has started laying away again.

I nearly forgot: our Sister Annunziata spent many years in that part of the world and she says watch out for the snakes with the zigzag markings. Most of the others are fine.

Best wishes from us all,
Sister B.

2

OPENING DAY

Dear Wanderer in the Peruvian Hinterlands,

We have passed your wonderful photograph round in awe for several days. The views from the high passes are extraordinary, aren't they? Nobody appreciates a mountain like a Fenlander. The nearest thing we have to a hill is a dual carriageway overpass in one direction and the bulldozed slopes of a landfill site in the other. As old Mr Rudd from the village said when he came back from his first holiday in the Lake District last year: "That's flat round here, that is."

Well, dear, the opening of the Shoppe is accomplished. I turned my sign to "open", I put on my new apron, I counted my float of £7.34 (hoping it was enough, it was all we had to hand) into the till and I waited. It was quite a long wait. I swept the floor again. I polished the window. I counted out the float again and made sure it was written in the float book. I checked several times that the sign did say "open", in case it had twisted round. It did; it hadn't. I was three whole rosaries in when finally a young man in a suit and oddly pointed shoes stepped in.

He smiled shyly and said "Hello. I've been sent to check out the new shop." I wondered if he was from Tesco, but he said, "I'm from the company called Intermediax in the offices up there in Odge's Lodge. We're only five minutes away." He looked around. "Is it just potatoes you sell then?"

I showed him our broad beans and our eggs. "We will be expanding our stock," I said, and because my mentor says every customer is a resource, and must always be listened to, I asked if there was anything else he would like in his new nearest shop.

"Milk, coffee, tea, biscuits," he said, "sugar." I wrote it down. "A nice variety of biscuits; some of them chocolate. Hobnobs, preferably."

I said, "Hobnobs?"

"It's a kind of biscuit," he explained. "You haven't done this before, have you? Office life can't function without biscuits. Especially in accounts!"

"Right!" I said. "We'll have them in stock by tomorrow." It was rash, but I felt I needed to rise to the challenge.

"Well," he said. "See you tomorrow then."

He hesitated at the door. "I'm Brian, by the way."

I went over and shook his hand. "Sister Boniface. Most people call me Sister B. Thank you, Brian, for being so helpful."

"I didn't actually buy anything, though. Sorry about that."

"But next time you will. And you'll tell your colleagues about the new shop and the Bobnobs."

"Hobnobs. Yes, I'll let them know."

And that, Sister, was my first customer. I was pondering the little list he had left me when in came Morris Odge, our neighbour. He is a tweedy farmer who drives huge vehicles – even his ordinary car has the look of a tractor – and usually has a flurry of terriers around his wellington boots.

He strode in braying, "Morning, Sister Boniface! Don't mind if I have a look, do you? The parish council, you know, is delighted by the shop. Just what we need. Village needs a shop. Now let me see." He scrutinised the stock with one eyebrow raised. "You're a bit sparse, aren't you?"

Feeling by now a little defensive I said I was expecting the wholesaler.

"Well," said Odge, "there are forty-odd workers over in the business units, most of them are young and hungry. At lunchtime they like a little stroll and this is just the right distance. Desk workers, you see. A few sandwiches and drinks and they'll be queuing up. Dog food would be good too. We're always running out of that at home. And cakes. Well, good luck to you. I'll take half a dozen eggs."

And that was my first sale. I rang £1.42 up on the till – *ching!* I gave Odge the correct change, as if I did it every day of my life and it was nothing special at all. I gave him his receipt and his eggs in a proper (recycled) box.

"You should charge more for these," he said on his way out. "Bye, Sister."

He was passed on the threshold by a wiry man, all bustling energy, in a brown grocer's coat.

"Right!" said this man and rubbed his hands together. He surveyed the Shoppe from left to right with a piercing eye. "Hedgeby," he said, "I'm from the wholesalers. We talked on the phone. Hari Menon recommended me." He produced a big order book from his pocket. He licked his pencil. "Right. Fire away, Sister! You start, and I'll make a few suggestions. We'll fill these shelves in no time sharp."

I'm glad to say that Rev Mother happened by soon after because I was quite overpowered by the range of even the most straightforward products – Hedgeby had six kinds of ginger biscuit and eleven types of washing-up liquid – but with her help we had, I reckoned, by lunchtime, something to tempt everyone in the parish, and their dogs. There are six varieties of milk. I thought milk was milk, but that just shows how out of touch I was. At Fenbiz they call it a steep learning curve. And how much of anything to order is anyone's guess.

"Ah!" said Hedgeby, with a sigh of professional satisfaction. "Stock control! Don't worry Sister, I'll see you right."

So by the end of the first day's trading I had gone from four product lines to about a hundred and from empty shelves to full ones; the exact opposite to what I had expected. Now all I need to do is to sell it all.

Best wishes,
Sister B.

3

BOUND!

Dear Sister Emelda,

It was a joy and a pleasure to hear the adventures of your trek over the mountains. The indigenous Peruvians sound as if they made you very welcome, as always. Your sketches were a delight, though a little rumpled thanks to a misfeed at the sorting office. Our postman, Wilf, says they're piloting a new machine, though why they should pilot a new Austrian high-tech sorting device at Littleport post office is a bit of a mystery.

I don't suppose it compares to your adventures trekking through virgin rainforests, but I've had a busy week here. Before the Shoppe opened I imagined having plenty of time to say a few rosaries between weighing out potatoes and beans, but a week of dealing with an enthusiastic wholesaler and that odd creature the General Public, and I realise I was probably wrong.

Mr Hedgeby's recent tactic has been to present us with free samples, so that we may test his wares at the convent and consider whether they are suitable for our little enterprise. Suitable, that is, in that they do not bring with them any temptation to lure our flock of customers into sin. This rules out premium strength lager and scratch cards, which my shop-keeping mentor, Mr Menon, strongly recommended in the Basic Retail classes I attended last term. Since luxury goods are too expensive for the Three Fens area and the supermarkets have cornered the market in cheap food, we are having to invent ourselves what they call a "niche market" here at St Winifreda's.

Last week Mr Hedgeby's sample was Bound!, a type of fabric conditioner which takes the form of handkerchief-sized sheets of what looks like poor quality rice paper. These are put in with laundry as it dries and are supposed to leave it soft and perfumed. Lady Celia recycled us a tumble drier last November, after she re-fitted the laundry at Cuffley Grange, so Sister Lucy added the pungent hankies to the laundry straight away. The smell is extraordinary; dolly mixtures and carbolic with a hint of hot elastic. It permeates the very walls of the convent, which having stood unperfumed for a couple of centuries, are not, in my opinion, in any way improved by it. The wretched smell is now never more than six inches from our nostrils (four inches in the case of Sister Emily).

We discussed Bound! and its place in the Shoppe at Wednesday convocation. Sister Lucy announced solid approval and wanted to pass on to the next item immediately. I waited for the others to take her up, but no-one did. Apparently all the sisters were as fond of Bound! as she. It makes ironing easier, apparently, and reduces static cling. No one was actually able to tell me what static cling was, but obviously it is highly undesirable and must be reduced.

"But the smell!" I objected.

"What smell?" they asked.

"The awful carbolic-y, dolly-mixture-ish smell we're all drenched in!" I cried.

They looked nonplussed. Finally Sister Bernard suggested that as I was not happy with Spring Fields, perhaps Woodland Ways would be more to my liking. Was it my imagination or was there some implied criticism of my character in this? Does she see me as more a creature of dim enclosed places than open, sunny meadows? I let it pass.

Onto the shelves, then, went Bound!, its awful essence getting into the carrots and, unless I'm much mistaken, into the baked beans as well. I waited for customer feedback, confident that the good people of Hog Fen and Low Lode would reject it with the contempt level-headed country people usually show newfangled extravagances. But I had reckoned without Lady Celia. She swept up in the Range Rover and carried off three boxes of the stuff assuring me it was the only thing for overpowering the smell of wet dogs at this time of year and she couldn't live without it. So it seems the fabric of Cuffley Grange is conditioned by Bound! as well as that of the convent.

Mrs Odge overheard and that was recommendation enough for her and now everyone in the parish has a box except old Mr Rudd, who is, I'm afraid, a lost cause in terms of laundry products and doomed to live for ever with his static cling.

Now I must go and pray for patience and for the pre-Easter rush of customers so often complained of at Tesco to spill over just a little and bring the week's profit up to double figures. I'm also hoping the Lord will somehow grant me escape from this awful smell.

Happy Easter and fondest regards,
Sister B.

4

SISTER CARMELLA

Dear Bringer of the Good News to Far Flung Places,

Naturally St Winifreda's Farm Shoppe (the spelling had nothing to do with me, we have a public relations sub-committee; I often have to pray for patience) remained firmly closed over most of Easter itself, so I have been able to dedicate myself to my devotions, apart from whitewashing the outhouse between the Vigil and Evensong last night.

It was on my way back to clean the brushes that I discovered poor Sister Carmella slumped over her wheelbarrow among the brassicas. She was feverish and quite unable to walk, and as all the others were at prayer or cooking there was nothing for it but to pile her into the barrow and wheel her to the infirmary. Luckily it has a ramp since Sister Mary Martyr had her hip replacement. Doctor Byfleet was called and arrived in paint-splashed overalls.

"Sorry to bother you, doctor," said Eustacia, our nurse.

"Not at all, Sister, it was a lucky escape – I was about to start on the ceiling. Dawn'll have to do it now!"

Doctor Byfleet may be the only doctor in the country who still makes house calls. He once told Eustacia that with six children, house calls were his only chance of a bit of peace.

No sooner had he stepped in to see Carmella than he put his head back out of the door and said, "I'm going to need a translator." Mother Eustacia and I looked at each other in surprise and blankly back at the doctor. "She doesn't speak very good English, does she?" he explained.

"Does she not?" said Eustacia. "Is that so? Well I never!"

"Didn't you know?"

"Well, the sister is quite new. She'll only have been here, well, how long is it now, Boniface?"

I did a quick calculation, calling to mind that Carmella had come to us from Warsaw around the time my first nephew was born.

"About fourteen years," I said.

The doctor looked surprised. "She doesn't seem to have a word of English, but perhaps it's just the fever," and he went back in to tend to her.

Eustacia and I then tried to recall when either of us had last heard Sister Carmella speak in English, or any other language. Opportunities for conversation are easily avoided, and some sisters express their calling very largely through silence, so it was not at all easy. Carmella definitely sang regularly in chapel. She went to confession, of course, but it was not right to speculate about that. Consequently, when he announced a bad case of flu and came back out to write her a prescription, we were able to add nothing to the doctor's information.

I walked him to his car. On the way he said, "Can it be possible for one of your sisters to live here for so long and not to have a conversation with anyone? It seems most unhealthy, psychologically, if you will excuse me saying so. How would you know if she were unhappy, for example?"

As he said this we were passing Sister Carmella's strawberry patch, I pointed to it and to the asparagus beyond and said that I doubted whether someone who could grow such healthy produce could be tormented, psychologically or any other way.

He gave me an odd look, accepted a dozen eggs for his trouble, and left.

But there may be something in what he says. Tomorrow I will take a dictionary and attempt to see how Sister Carmella is in body and in psyche. My guess is that she will be impatient both with my beginner's Polish and with any ailment that keeps her away from the planting.

In full hopes of your latest journey being safely accomplished,

Best wishes,
Sister B.

5

COMMUNITY SERVICE

Dear Traveller,

Sister Carmella is much recovered and as fluent in English as she needs to be to issue long lists of instructions. It fell to me to pass these on to the community service workers yesterday. They first came on the recommendation of the Poor Claires. The Claires, as you know, are a very holy order who don't wear shoes, which makes gardening difficult for them. Not talking is another of their forms of worship, but it does not stop them writing letters – scarcely a day passes without a long note from one of them.

Where was I? Ah yes, thanks to the Claires we took on our first community service workers last year, despite dire warnings from the more pessimistic sisters. They come with Ted, their long-suffering supervisor, whose job is to keep them hard at it in the right protective clothing for the correct number of hours. For insurance reasons they must wear protective goggles, boots, gloves and, as the job requires, sometimes ear protectors and masks as well. On a good day they look as if they are about to tackle one of Sellafield's riskier projects.

Sister Carmella and our other gardening sisters, I need hardly tell you, have no protective clothing other than wellies. Carmella still even wears the long habit. Ted sucks his teeth in disapproval whenever he sees this, but has given up asking about our insurance position since we explained about the Lord offering us all the cover we needed (and could afford).

Yesterday Ted had two of his regulars, Animal and Baz, with him, along with a new worker, Alphonsus. Animal and Baz are an odd couple; Baz being a thin, pale, fidgety boy and Animal vast, loud and lumbering. Alphonsus looks like Shelley, with violinist's hands and the type of accent not regularly heard since Princess Margaret. He told me immediately that he was a computer hacker. Ted does not encourage conversation with the workers. It makes them, as he puts it, "too philosophical" so I set them to work re-roofing the tool-shed and left.

Over lunch I mentioned to Sister Bernard, our choir mistress and computer technician, about Alphonsus and his hacking. Her eyes lit up. "I wonder if he could sort out the PC's problems?" she said. "I bet he's the one I read about. Is his name Dunn, Alphonsus Dunn?"

I didn't know, but it seemed likely. Dunn, she told me, was famous for having illegally connected himself to the Inland Revenue's computer and arranged for it to issue him refund cheques. He did not do this for personal gain – or so he said – but to prove that the Inland Revenue had wasted millions on a computer system that was poorly designed and insecure.

"The *Daily Mail* called him the Hacker with a Heart," Sister Bernard told me. "And it's true about the Revenue's computer system being a failure, they admitted it."

As we left the refectory, Sister Bernard slipped off to the chapel to pray for guidance. If the Lord has sent Alphonsus to us for a special purpose, then she means to discover it.

Meanwhile, I returned to the vegetable garden to find Animal and Baz busy roofing, but Alphonsus on "official rest". Official rest is when Ted says you can stop; unofficial rest is when you lean on your spade and get philosophical. Alphonsus was having to rest because he was not used to the outdoor work and had come over faint on the ladder. Ted was wondering whether he ought to be wearing a hard hat, and whether he might have to stay behind on the envelope stuffing team next week if he wasn't up to outdoor duty.

Over tea and biscuits, the only hospitality we are allowed to give them, I heard Animal and Baz giving Alphonsus their advice.

Animal: "You don't want to do that indoor stuff, you never know who they'll have on envelope stuffing."

Baz: "It's for funny people. The ones who can't be allowed out, sort of thing." (A lot of nodding and tapping of the nose accompanied this).

Alphonsus looked puzzled, carefully pouring hot water onto the mint teabag he had brought with him.

"I suppose it might be rather dull," he said finally.

"Dull?" said Animal. "No, not dull – dodgy!"

"Yeah," Baz agreed, palming three chocolate biscuits from the plate at once. "Dodgy. It's only the funny ones they keep indoors. Pervs, mostly."

"Pervs and smackheads."

"Only the bad smackheads," Baz pointed out reasonably. "The not-so-bad-ones can still do a bit of proper work."

"True," Animal agreed, "they're not much good, though. Remember Thin Jim? He couldn't remember anything you said. He'd go off to get something, then come back three times and ask what it was. Talk about useless!"

They laughed merrily, but Alphonsus still seemed puzzled.

"It was the drugs, see?" Baz explained. "They do your head in."

"And you should know!" Animal said, with a hint of admiration.

"Yeah, I should know. Listen, old mate, you're a lot better off with us. You don't want to stuff envelopes with a load of weirdos. We'll keep an eye on you."

"Come on, lads, that's twenty minutes. Back to work," Ted called from outside, where he had been checking the ladder.

They went back to the roofing, and Alphonsus – he's always called that, not even Animal and Baz seem tempted to shorten his name – was sent inside to sort and clear up the tools. When I returned to sign them off at the end of the day the roof was completed, and inside the jumble of tools, pots, seed packets and sacks had been tidied as no one had ever tidied it before. Forks were in order of tine length, pots stacked left to right by size and width, and all the seeds were in alphabetical order.

Sister Carmella will either be delighted or infuriated by this, you can never tell with gardeners.

The blessing of the Lord be with you out there,

Best wishes,
Sister B.

21

6

CHOCOLATE

Dear Sister Emelda,

I have just looked up your latest address on the internet, and it said: "It is a vast modern city which has grown out of control. It does not have clean water for all of its inhabitants, its sanitary system does not exist in poor neighbourhoods, and even its electrical grid is not sufficient to meet the needs of the city." God bless you, dear Wanderer. Nobody could accuse you of taking life easy!

I have been rather slow to reply to your last letter, because we have had that joyful thing: a sudden increase in customers! I put this down to confectionery. Until last week I had resisted all Mr Hedgeby's attempts to persuade me to stock sweets. We are a farm shop, not a confectioner's, I reasoned. We sell vegetables, a few basic groceries and household cleaning products – sensible, practical things, not chocolate, definitely.

But on Wednesday Mr Hedgeby said, "Tell you what, Sister, what if I was to leave one little box on trial, here near the till? Just one. It's fair trade. And if nobody buys, I'll take it away next week, no questions asked. Whatjersay?"

Well, what I was about to say was, "Thank you, but no. There's no demand."

But before I could, in came Alphonsus Dunn on his break, and he said, "Ah, chocolate, spot on. Three bars please, Sister."

And as I rang that up, there followed a pair of young men in suits from Odge's business units and they bought milk and sugar and said, "Oh great, a couple of bars of chocolate too. No, make that four bars, the girls love it." So that was seven bars out of the box of ten sold inside three minutes.

Mr Hedgeby could hardly contain himself. His eyebrows were positively dancing.

So I gave in and now the Shoppe sells three types of fair trade chocolate and footfall's up thirty-five per cent.

Alphonsus is around quite a lot now. Carmella was stunned by the tidiness of her shed, and we all felt that work could easily be found for a young man of such fastidious habits, even if he couldn't go up ladders. He's pricked out nearly four hundred bedding plants in the greenhouse so far and whenever I pass he is humming away to Radio 3, which he can play somehow on his mobile telephone. Every now and then Sister Bernard pops in and, under cover of stacking spare pots or carrying in a bag of compost, picks his brain over computer technicalities.

Last time I passed he was saying, "Well, de-fragging the hard disk might be worth a try…" Don't ask me what that's about, but there's definitely talk of a website and Alphonsus is to be its maker.

"Now is that wise?" I asked at convocation. "He's a likeable boy, but he's got a criminal record for computer things. He might put a virus in the website and use it to Trojan the Whitehouse or something. Then where would we be?"

"Have you been reading *What Computer* again?" someone asked. "You know it gives you funny ideas. Trojaning the White House indeed!" They all laughed.

Sisters who I know for a certain fact have never touched a computer and wouldn't know a USB from their elbow chuckled merrily and dismissed me as a dreadful cynic, implying that I distrusted a poor innocent lad quite unreasonably.

Oh dear, looking back, perhaps I did. For shame. Anyway, Alphonsus can apparently whip us up a website in no time, we can check absolutely every word before it goes on public view, *and* we can use it to advertise special offers in the Shoppe. I still need a little persuading that my customers are going to look on a website before they come for their milk or their bars of free trade chocolate, but who am I to cavil? I just run the place.

Oh dear, please pray for my patience and my obedience, dear sister.

Best wishes,
Sister B.

7
A NEW NOVICE

Dear Fearless Traveller in the Lord's Work,

Rev Mother bounded into the Shoppe this morning with a letter and said, "Boniface, the Bishop's financial adviser is coming tomorrow to check some of our paperwork. Can we run to a few biscuits?"

I said of course, and recommended Hobnobs, which my shop keeping experience has told me are the biscuit of choice for business people – although on reflection an older canon may prefer the more traditional Bourbon.

"In France," Rev Mother remarked, examining the packets, "they have local biscuits and local cakes, don't they? I definitely remember little *gallettes de Saint Audin* in Normandy and a *gateau Mont Delou* – meringue I think that was. Perhaps we should devise our very own type of biscuit: *Hobnobbe de Sainte Winifrede*, something like that! I'll leave the details to you, dear. Anyway, I'll take these. And if you see Hermione, could you ask her to come over and help me get the papers ready? He wants all sorts of titles and deeds as well as the ledgers."

Hermione is our new novice. We are very pleased to have a new novice. She is actually the first proper one we've had since 1996. She impressed us all by being tall enough to clear the outbuilding gutters without a ladder.

"Brilliant to have someone tall onboard, and a trained bookkeeper and archivist too – we've hit the jackpot with you, Hermione," Rev Mother said when she was introduced. "Oh, and of course someone of your spiritual qualities."

Hermione blushed so much she steamed up her glasses. She is from Torquay and cycled here – a fair test of commitment in itself. Her main task, when she is not sorting out papers for diocesan financial advisers, is to research and write a history of the Little Sisters of St Winifreda-in-the-Fen. This was Rev Mother's brainwave. We have piles and piles of ancient papers, and people often ask about our history. So, as the Good Lord has sent us an archivist, it seems the time has come to sort it all out and get it down on paper.

When she had finished putting up beanpoles with the CS workers, I asked Hermione why she thought the Bishop's office suddenly wanted so much information.

"It said in the letter it was part of a review," she told me. "I think they might be trying to work out how much St Winifreda's costs. We've asked for some money for repairs, especially to the bell tower and the roof, and I imagine they're wondering how much it's all going to come to."

The bell tower needs a little more than a repair, really. First it developed a crack. We hadn't really noticed until Farmer Odge squinted at it one day last month on his way back to the car and said, "Boniface, I swear the top of that tower's leaning. It never leaned like that before."

We both stood and peered at it. It was hard to say, but as we watched a chunk of something – a bit of gargoyle or a piece of mortar – fell off and bounced into the lane.

"If something like that hits a car, or a person, it'll be serious. You'd better get someone up there to look at it soonest." Odge said.

To be honest, Emelda, we've all known there was trouble with the tower for some time. It's a funny old thing, a gift in the mid-19th century from a neighbouring aristocrat whose whole family survived a bout of typhus. She was an eccentric woman and wealthy enough for it to show, so she had it designed by a pupil of Pugin, the one who did the Houses of Parliament. It is as ornate and neo-gothic as can be. There are dozens of gargoyles of the most lurid and monstrous kind grimacing down at us day in, day out, and at forty-five feet it's the highest building between here and Ely cathedral; members of our little order have always found a bit too prominent.

It might have been stylish in its day, but it was never well-constructed and has been developing cracks and leaks from the very first. Stone ornaments the size of large pickled onions regularly plummet to earth. Since 1902, when a whole griffon's head landed too near a visiting Dominican, we hardly use it, except as a giant letterbox (it stands between the main convent buildings and the road). Apart from that, its only use is to ring out the departing souls of our sisters. Its bell has a lovely chime.

At convocation we wondered about a surveyor. Should we? We guessed at least £100 and felt fairly sure they would bring nothing but bad news, so we agreed instead to pray, and to make sure to point out the leaning tower (well, the one in Pisa has lasted long enough) to the Bishop's man. We can always count on the diocese for help, when it comes to it.

Meanwhile I am left with Rev Mother's biscuit challenge. What do you think? Fenland Fingers? Convent Crumbles? All ideas welcome.

Best wishes,
Sister B.

8

Mr Wooler's Visit

Dear Emelda,

We loved your class's ideas for biscuit names and look forward to selling St. Winifreda's Armadillo, Llama and Guinea Pig biscuits very soon.

Speaking of biscuits with odd names, I've been sending Garibaldis over to Mr Wooler in the library all week. When he arrived on Monday he handed Hermione a note. She read it to Rev Mother and me in the Shoppe. It said, "Mr Wooler requires coffee at 9.10 am, 10.30 am and 11.45 am. At 1.30 pm he takes soup and a brown roll at his desk. At 3 pm and 4.20 pm he takes tea. Both tea and coffee should be white with no sugar. Biscuits should be provided with all hot drinks, preferably Garibaldi or similar."

"Well, I suppose it's clear, at least," said Rev Mother. "We'd better do as he asks even if he does seem to have mistaken us for his handmaidens."

Hermione, as his designated assistant, bore the brunt of both the food and drink legwork and the complaints. Our records are not what he had hoped for.

"He keeps asking for deeds and wills. The accounts are in perfect order, but he hasn't even glanced at them. It's the old papers he wants to look at and they're in a terrible jumble, not sorted at all, just piled into the screened reading room at the end. You can hardly get in."

"I was warned about that," Rev Mother said. "Our dear predecessors were too busy with their prayers and scraping a bare living to concern themselves with paperwork. A fair number of them were illiterate too. Uneducated but holy. One can only admire…"

"Well it's Mr Wooler's worst nightmare," Hermione told us. "He can't work out who owns what, so he can't tell what can be sold. We are the worst case he's ever seen. Even at the Marian convent in Woolwich he found the deeds with no trouble."

"Yes. That's a Holiday Inn now, I believe." said Rev Mother. "This isn't at all what I was expecting. I thought Mr Wooler would meet us and make interesting suggestions about how we can improve our finances. I hoped for bright strategic ideas, not asset stripping. I shall have to pray for guidance. Meanwhile, Hermione, I suggest you take him his refreshments and help him in small ways only."

"That won't be difficult." Hermione sighed. "He expects very little of me. Reaching things down from the top shelf has been my most demanding assignment to date. And he expects me to stir his tea!"

Three days and two packets of biscuits later, Mr Wooler left, telling us to expect his report and indicating that he was very disappointed with both the record-keeping and the assets he had found at St Winifreda's. A walnut-sized chunk of brickwork fell from the tower as he passed and bounced off the bonnet of his gleaming car. From the Shoppe I could see him shout and dance with rage. Luckily none of us was within earshot.

Best wishes,
Sister B

9

GREENING WITH DOCTOR ROD

Dear Deliverer of the Good News to Far Flung Places,

How marvellous to receive your last letter, even if it did take six weeks. I understand, of course, about the problem of stamps in the remoter parts of the Andes. I think the delay at the King's Lynn end was something to do with the excess postage charge of £14.17. Luckily Wilf, our postman, forgot his glasses again so we can pay later, and profits in the Shoppe are into two figures this week because of our new environmental credentials (about which more later).

Meantime, I am stumped by your ethical query. I can quite see that in order to share the insights of the Shaman, it may be necessary to puff on the special pipe, but how often and whether or not to inhale seems to be outside the normal St Winifreda's guidelines. I'll pass the matter on to Rev Mother, but I'm afraid she's very preoccupied with "greening" the convent at present.

Most days she is deep in conference with Doctor Rod, the energy efficiency consultant. They talk about planning sites for reed beds, windmills and renewable woodlands for coppicing. I am all in favour, obviously, but grimly aware that on a budget of £0.00, any actual construction work will probably fall to Sister Bernard, Sister Maria Celeste, Sister Mary Loyola and myself. We are all agile and willing, but I keep thinking back to the septic tank incident.

Rod was sent to us by the Lord last year. His email coincided with our new Rev Mother's arrival and, as she said, it dovetailed perfectly with item three (energy sustainability) on her Future of St Winifreda's Plan! Aerial photography apparently showed him and his team from the university that this was an absolutely perfect site for experiments in rural energy self-sufficiency. He pitched up with a minibus of graduate students and set about a feasibility study – all free – because they need the practice.

He is small and very broad with tattoos on his calves (he always wears shorts and boots). As you know, Rev Mother is tall and lean; from a distance they look like Don Quixote and Sancho Panza, especially as they wave their arms about whenever they think of the turbine possibilities.

Big discussion over supper tonight about whether sunblock is compatible with the religious life. Many of us have been so long covered that any tiny exposure to sun burns us instantly. Sister Carmella rolls up her sleeves when gardening sometimes and has freckles the size of ten pence pieces to the elbow. Sister Adelaide, who visited last year from (you guessed!) Australia, read us all lectures about ozone layer shrinkage leading to skin cancer, and she never went out without painting her face like a test cricketer.

Some of the more nervous retired sisters began plastering their faces with zinc ointment, even though they never go outside at all, but Sister Eustacia said it was all foolish vanity and the whole planet's population needed to live with the mess we had made of the world and what happened to our skins was God's will anyway. Since sunblock is at least £5 a tube (I asked in the chemist on the last pre-scription run), I'm hoping she's right.

This week's big money-spinner at the Shoppe is environmentally friendly wellington boots. I have shifted no less than seven pairs to school run mums (a nice noun phrase I picked up from one of Mr Tetherton's tabloids). The boots are made from recycled car tyres in a sheltered workshop, so are bursting with ethical credibility and the ladies snapped them up. They usually just buy milk.

Yesterday one said, "I want cappuccino milk, actu-ally. For cappuccinos, you know? Do you have that?"

Now I have walked past enough hospital Costa Coffees to know what cappuccino is, but I had no idea in all heaven what she meant by cappuccino milk. However, Mr Menon advises prompt, definite and above all positive replies to all customer queries, so I assured her that whole milk was what she wanted and she bought four litres, just like that!

Wednesday

Another joyful day in the service of the Lord, dear sister. I know you sneeze at torrents and hurricanes with all your experience as a traveller, but I honestly think even you would be impressed by the weather here lately. About six inches of rain fell vertically between 6.30am and 8am this morning and now just coming up to Angelus it's boiling hot again.

It's very quiet around the building today because of the Whole Sisterhood Seminar called Ecumenism and You: the Long View. I have volunteered to man the Shoppe throughout – a considerable sacrifice in philosophical terms, but frankly a welcome relief in others. Sister Zofia has prepared one of her papers, and although she has worked long and hard on her English, the draft she kindly allowed me to read was still very, well, Albanian, and her idea of using the computer translation thingy had not helped one bit.

Nearly all the retired sisters have signed up for a workshop entitled Updating the Vulgar, on the basis, I fear, of a misunderstanding. But that never bothers Fr McMann who can do no wrong with the over-nineties on account of his ability to play "Tiptoe Through the Tulips" on the spoons. Many of the sisters will have nodded off by now; not the Ursulines though, they're in there revelling in the theological Hard Sums, as usual.

We have a small stand of newspapers and magazines in the Shoppe now. Customers like it and the Parish Council has officially enthused, but I have my doubts. For one thing, the tabloids (well, I needn't say more), for another, the terrifically addictive power of news. You start by glancing at the headlines and, before you know, it's an hour later and you're onto horoscopes and wedges versus kitten heels. I have imposed a personal five-minutes-a-day-front-pages-only rule. Despite this, I am developing sub-editor's disease, which is a dangerous tendency for Sun-style headlines to spring to mind.

I asked Mr Tetherton, who delivers our papers, whether he found the newspapers tempting, but he said after thirty-two years in the business he only bothered with Competition Carp.

A bit of a setback to report on the "green" wellies, unfortunately. They turn out to be made in China – still from recycled materials and so forth, but their carbon footprint (so to speak) turns out to be enormous because they have to ship them here in containers. Not at all the kind of thing we want to encourage in the carbon-friendly Shoppe. (SISTERS SHOCKED BY GIANT "GREEN" WELLY FOOTPRINT.)

We can at least congratulate ourselves on recycling. There is hardly anything Sister Immaculate Claire of Siena can't save, re-process, re-purpose or send off for salvage. She has a very handy machine for compressing cans into building blocks and once you get used to them they make very striking retaining walls for the raised beds. Apparently the glass pulverised from old communion wine bottles can be used for insulation and old newspapers can be reprocessed into warm fleece jackets – or was it the other way round? She was able to report on Thursday that we had far outstripped the Tokyo Summit Targets, which is nice because leading the world is something this part of East Anglia can only rarely claim to have done (except perhaps in modesty).

One piece of great news: Dr Rod's energy survey pointed out that tumble driers are not our ecological friends. Ours was sent straight off to the charity re-sale centre – and the smell of Bound! went with it. (OUT WITH BOUND!) Hurrah!

Good luck in the mountains. Prayer is pretty much your only recourse on the narrowest paths, Sister Annunziata tells me.

Yours,
Sister B.

10

SPECIAL WHITE DUST

Dear Traveller in the Lord,

I write in haste with only a few moments to spare between the convocation and late prayers. No surprise that the meeting lasted this long; it was destined to run and run with item one being Rev Mother's report on her Future of the Religious Life Conference in Cologne (eternal) and item two, the television debate: round six, pensioners v. Ursulines.

St Winifreda's has over the years become a centre for sisters of many orders, denominations and even faiths. We have what Rev Mother calls the inclusive/ eclectic approach. Indeed she is a great advocate of it and recently addressed a conference (Stirring the Pot: Absolute Diversity: Benefits, Duties, Rewards!) on the issue in Ely.

As a result we are twinned with holy houses the world over, which gave us good reason to hang a world map in the meeting room and stick a pin in it wherever we had contacts. I am proud to tell you it fairly bristles, Emelda! We welcome religious women from all over and are very proud of our open door tradition. The convent's retirement home, the Father Edward Wilson Centre, houses a spirited mix of more than twenty sisters of advanced years – very advanced indeed in some cases – and a great many nationalities. Recently one of them was presented with a television set by a relative.

We had lived cheerfully without one until then, but no sooner was it connected than the great debate began. I will not trouble you with a full account; suffice to say that tonight the Ursulines (ever a liberal group, even into their nineties), who favour complete de-regulation, mounted a strong challenge to Srs Mary Martyr and Ignatius, of the 6-10 pm, BBC Only party. There was no debate, as such, of course, our rule allows only a brief statement and then we have silent prayer until a consensus is reached; or not reached, in which case we put the item back on the list for next week and offer it three times a day for intercession.

"Not much chance of a satellite dish in time for the Champions League whichever way you look at it," Sister Eustacia remarked on the way out.

Personally I can't abide the thing. I have trouble enough with Radio 4; whenever my back's turned for five minutes I seem to miss another Big Event in *The Archers*. This is because they time the Big Archers Events to coincide with the Big Religious Festivals. One could almost suspect BBC management of acting without a single thought for the members of religious orders among their audience. I would e-mail in protest if we could make the computer work.

But these are worldly matters and we must not allow them to occupy our thoughts for long, as Father Humbert so often reminded us in his Lenten addresses this year. He lost his voice after the first three, but we had his theme by then. Item three on the agenda this evening took less than a minute. We decided to return to our practice of inviting a guest speaker for Lent next year. A Benedictine, we thought – they're always good value and tend to smoke less than the Franciscans.

This afternoon saw a sorry setback to our plans to sell organic produce in the Shoppe. This is a great disappointment as organic potatoes are (if you'll excuse a moment's weakness) so much more desiree and so much more profitable. Frankly, they formed the keynote of my cash projections for the coming two quarters.

The man from the Soil Association came and was as hearty, bearded and corduroyed as you might expect. He heaped admiration on the tilth and friability of Carmella's beds, praised her husbandry and ran his fingers through her compost with a sigh of pleasure, but blenched and grew gruff when he came across her special mix in the biscuit tin in the shed.

"You wouldn't be using this on the soil, by any chance?" he asked.

"Oh, yes," said Rev Mother, who was giving him the tour. "Carmella prepares this herself."

Our Soil Association visitor sniffed warily at the tin. "What is it?"

"It kills thistles and carrot root fly as well," Rev Mother said with pride. "She mixes it herself. We just call it her special white dust."

"I'm afraid you may have misunderstood some of the principles of organic gardening," he said. And with that he tucked his clipboard under his arm and left. So no stamp of approval for us.

I dread to think what Mr Menon will say when I tell him. It's nothing short of potato price wars round here – three farmers in our area are loss leading with homegrown spuds by the sack for under £2 at the gate. I was so hoping organic status would give us the edge!

The new artisan bread maker from Bardisham came by and left us a fragrant basketful of samples to try. I can't imagine many of our regulars branching out into exotic bread, but I gave some to the Community Service workers in return for consumer feedback. Animal ate three rolls at once, grinned and gave a thumbs up sign as he chewed; Baz gnawed a seeded roll with a frown of fierce concentration and declared it the best thing he'd ever tasted in his whole life; and Alphonsus said the combination of rye and spelt lent it a hearty texture and a deliciously yeasty flavour, with the hint of oregano adding a very appealing touch of the Mediterranean. It is expensive, but Mr Menon assures me the market is ready to pay a premium for handcrafted goods, so I have ordered a few loaves to see if he's right. £2.45 apiece.

"We're not in *Islington*, Sister!" Mrs Odge remarked when she saw the price.

We must pray for guidance, on this matter and all else.

With God's blessings,
Sister B.

11

A STRANGE YOUNG CUSTOMER

Dear Wanderer,

I do sympathise with the sunburn and dehydration, but am having some difficulty imagining the trials of a sunny climate. Rainfall in these parts is reaching Old Testament levels. The Ouse has oozed over its banks and the water meadows beyond the kitchen garden walls are all water and no meadow. Our forebears were canny women and built on the only bit of higher land for miles around, so we are not flooded, except for the big leak in the roof of the refectory and a few lesser ones in the dormitories (the ones not already shut because of damp).

The weather has kept people at home. Today my customer-throughput consisted of Mrs Odge, who tutted over the price of tea bags, Mr Hedgeby with samples of oven cleaner and Five Fruit drink without tartrazine (I believe this is a good thing), and an odd teenager who visits most days, but has yet to commit to any purchase.

She is a thin, underdressed girl of about sixteen with a lot of earrings. She wanders in, hands fisted in jacket pockets, always looking cold and wet, casts a penetrating glance left to right over the stock and then utters her ritual challenge: "Got any Cheesy Wotsits?" or some other brand name which means absolutely nothing to me. She has done this most days for the past three weeks.

Mr Hedgeby thinks I should move into fancy goods. By fancy goods he tells me he means local honey and homemade fudge. The wholesalers do a good line in homemade fudge and he can buy in local honey from London. Then there's the possibility of filled rolls and baguettes.

Oh how prone to temptation is the Shoppe proprietor faced with such enticements! But Sister Gertrude in the kitchen is more at home with root vegetables than French loaves and I will have to plan how to broach the roll-filling, as she is pretty well flat-out, and the old cooking range is getting terribly arthritic. From the Shoppe I sometimes hear a terrible sort of Samurai shout – "Haieee!" – followed by a hefty metallic clang, which is poor Gertrude kicking the oven door closed.

On a happier note, we celebrate Sister Bernard's Saint's day today. She is hoping for a modem dongle, and I happen to know, as the one in charge of the collection, that she will not be disappointed. I ordered it yesterday and it has just been delivered by a youth in a helmet. It seems to be assumed that people ordering computer equipment need it rushed to them by someone on a motorbike. Rather exciting, I must admit, but not really necessary, particularly if, as in our case, the power supply is off due to damp wiring. If one could choose anything to be rushed to us covered in Urgent Delivery stickers it would be a large roll of roofing felt filled with an energetic team of charitably-minded roof repairers.

Yours in hope,
Sister B.

12

NESBITT

Dear Pilgrim,

I am reminded, not for the first time, of how swift and how oblique the answer to prayer can be. No sooner had I asked for assistance with the roof than I was sent an assistant for the Shoppe. Her name is Nesbitt. I think I mentioned the girl before – she had been coming in daily asking for things I had never heard of.

Until last week I had simply replied that we didn't stock Pickled Onion Monster Munch, Cherry Tango, Nachos with Blue Cheese, or whatever the item happened to be and offered an alternative, such as a cauliflower, or a nice sliced loaf. But finally I put a little plan into action. I bought a new line from Mr Hedgeby, hid the box under the counter and the next time, when she demanded, "Got any Doctor Pepper?" I said no, but I did have some Kit-Kats.

Taken aback by this, she made eye contact for the first time. "I'll have two then. One for my brother."

She paid up, unwrapped and munched on the spot, then, seemingly restored to social function by the chocolate, introduced herself between mouthfuls.

"I'm Nesbitt."

I told her my name and carried on bagging potatoes.

"You'd be a nun, then," Nesbitt went on.

I said I was, yes.

"D'you have to be a nun to work here?"

I said I didn't think there was a rule about it either way.

"You want to take somebody on. Somebody to tell you the right stuff to get in. The school bus stops near here, you know."

I told her we couldn't possibly afford to pay anyone.

"Oh," she said, disappointed. "I'll have to think it over in that case."

The next day she arrived punctually at nine o' clock, wearing a brown overall many sizes too big. She told me she could only give me a couple of hours a week and then she started washing carrots. She washed them rather well. When Mr Hedgeby dropped in she had a few words with him and he left a large box of Cheesy Wotsits, a rainbow array of tins of fizzy drinks and assorted chocolate bars with strange, lively names like Snickers and Time Out. In ten minutes Nesbitt had arranged these into a professional display at the end of the counter near the till. Tomorrow the school term begins and she confidently expects a rush... We'll see.

Good luck in the mountains,
Sister B.

13

PURE AND SIMPLE

Dear blessed Wanderer,

A day spent bussing the infirm to the clinic and day centre enlivened by long waits at both with nothing to read but *Country House* magazine (September 1995) and, more fascinating still, *Ideal Homes* and *Lifestyle* (April 1996). Actually there was another magazine in the pile, called *GQ*.

Puzzled by what the initials could mean, I dived into an issue and soon became aware that it was not at all the sort of thing the rest of the people in the waiting room expected to see me reading. Spectacular feature on body piercing – poor boys! It must hurt dreadfully, and what must their mothers say? Most of them look as if they haven't seen a hot meal in the past month, perhaps they have spent all their money on having parts of themselves drilled and hung with cold little dumbbells.

It takes a while for the eye to accustom itself to the riotously busy and colourful layout of these publications. Their pages do bellow so at the reader.

Actual reading of the text is, I think, not being encouraged; more a dreamy scanning of the photographs and a gentle absorption of something that feels like information, but is actually something else. Just the thing for any NHS waiting room.

How one pities any poor householder trying to live up to the ideals of *Ideal Homes.* Not only must one be rich and/or quirkily creative, but one must absolutely have a dazzling house, a handsome spouse, several photogenic children and a characterful dog. It is not enough for the house to be designed to your own specification and furnished with items collected from all corners of the globe ("Natalie delights in the Thai temple masks, which she used as the basis of the colour scheme for her airy lounge/diner."), it must be located somewhere unusual: beside, or even in, a river; on a Hebridean isle or, at a pinch, in the heart of an inner city industrial zone, but rather a nice one, obviously.

I was interested to note, in a feature unflinchingly called How the Rich Live, that people with an unlimited budget often end up with a kitchen just like the one at the convent. Imagine that! Plain and simple is what they desire, and yet they send to Borneo for their light fittings.

By the time the sisters had finished with their assorted specialists I was right up to date on the Spice Girls' preferences in sofas. I look forward to mentioning Mel C's fondness for lemon yellow to Nesbitt in a casual way very soon.

I was late back to the Shoppe because unloading old nuns is tremendously slow, especially when they have been over-stimulated by the excitements of a day's medical attention.

When I finally arrived to cash up I found a note. It said "Takings=£32.45 need Mr Mars & Mr Muscle. See ya. N." Not quite what they teach in Business Letter Writing, but good enough.

Convocation this evening and unless I'm wrong Sister Bernard will be launching her bid for a permanent fixed aerial for the TV. The little wiry thing it came with offers a picture so grainy that even Jeremy Paxman looks insubstantial. And there's a big announcement from the Diocese, Rev Mother says.

Yours, in anticipation of a long evening,
Sister B.

14

A CARDBOARD TOWER

Dear Head Teacher of the brand new Los Santos
School,

Congratulations on the founding of the new
school, even if it is just an old desk under a big
tree at the moment. We are putting together a collection of second-hand books; they were clearing
out the public library and the Oxfam shop did us a
special deal. We will bundle them up with a few pens
and some paper and get them in the post as soon as
we can. I had a peep and some of the book titles (*Jill
Enjoys her Ponies, Fifth Form at Malory Towers*) may not
relate very closely to your students' experience there
in the remote jungles of Peru, but I'm sure they'll
still enjoy them. I did, and I never had a pony either.

And speaking of towers – I have just built one!
Only of cardboard, but rather magnificent. It stands
seven feet high and is a replica of St Winifreda's,
but without the cracks. This is our response to the
Bishop's financial advice. Rev Mother read us his letter at convocation.

"It is with the greatest regret," she read "that we must advise the sisterhood that running repairs to St Winifreda's have far outrun the usual budget. We can only advise self-sufficiency, fundraising and an informed assessment of any assets that might be liquidated. We shall, of course, continue to make the services of Mr Wooler available. He is an expert at realising potential funds and I have asked him on your behalf to put together a proposal for the future financial management of the convent that will include repairs to the capital asset."

"Is that a no, then?" asked Eustacia.

"It is," Rev Mother said. "That is to say we are advised to sell something or raise the money some other way."

"How much is the roof going to cost?" asked Agnes.

Rev Mother winced. She read from the letter. "The estimates here say about eighty thousand pounds."

We fell silent. The figure represented the profits of the Shoppe for a couple of centuries.

"Hermione," said Rev Mother. "I asked you to put together a list of the convent's assets. Have you had time?"

"Well, I've made a start," said Hermione, "but there are a couple of things...problems..."

"Well?"

"You see a lot of the papers are extremely old. It's hard to tell whether they still apply. We've been given all sorts of things over the years: pieces of land, grazing rights, rights to collect tolls…"

"Flannel petticoats," said Mother Hilda.

"Yes, lots of flannel petticoats," said Hermione. "They were a popular gift at one time. There's no way of telling whether we still own any of these things now. Not the flannel petticoats, obviously – I mean the land and things. Mr Wooler said most of the donations had been superseded or expired by now. There's still a huge pile of papers at the far end that I haven't got to yet, but so far there is no obvious source of funds. Sorry."

We prayed for a while.

"Um, one more thing, actually," Hermione said. We all looked. "It's just that, I don't know if it's any help, but we seem to have received a letter quite like that one from the diocese at least once every twenty years for the last three hundred years or so. There's a whole box of them. They all say more or less what this one says: there isn't enough money. Some are a lot worse, actually. They quite often threaten immediate closure. One threatens excommunication."

"Oh?" said Rev Mother. "What did the sisters do? How did they react to these letters?"

"They just seem to have put them into a box. In fact the box had "Mala" written on the side. I thought it was a name at first, but then realised it just means 'bad things'. They tucked anything they didn't care for in there and locked it. The excommunication letter was in there right at the bottom!"

Hermione glanced up from her papers and noticed our expressions. Her face changed. "Obviously you know all about this…"

"Did you say excommunication?"

"Surely you…you must have been aware…? She trailed off.

"You'd better tell us as plainly as you can," Rev Mother said. We all grabbed for our rosaries.

"I can't believe you didn't know…"

"Please, Hermione, just explain what you have found."

Hermione sat up bravely, flicked through her notebook until she found the right page, and began. "Well, Pius the Ninth declared the doctrine of Papal Infallibility in 1857 and in 1867 he ruled that anyone who denied papal infallibility must be excommunicated. Anyone at all. There seems to have been quite a long exchange of letters between St Winifreda's and the Diocese. It is quite an angry series of letters, actually, although obviously I've only read the ones St Winifreda received, and not the ones they sent. At one point the Bishop described St Winifreda's convent as, I quote, "that remote impoverished house of notorious women and wicked sisters". They were "outspoken, wilful and possessed of all manner of opinions that make them wholly unsuitable for inclusion among the blessed. By thought and deed they have shown themselves disobedient to the authority of Holy Mother Church and as such seem hardly fit to continue under its protection." The bishops fully supported the excommunication of all convents or monasteries that didn't immediately subscribe to the doctrine. They seem not to have liked the religious houses very much. They were a bit difficult to control. They tended to go their own ways. Quite a lot were excommunicated at that time. Others chose to leave and live independently."

"And St Winifreda's?" asked Rev Mother.

"Well, it isn't quite clear. The letter, as I say, was just there at the bottom of the box, but subsequent letters sound as if the convent was still answerable to the diocese and received some support, so I guess it just blew over. I'm sorry. I assumed this must be well known to you all."

"Presumably there are other letters confirming that this threat to excommunicate was just a technicality…" Rev Mother said, in a keep calm sort of voice.

"I'm guessing there are, but I haven't got to them yet," Hermione said. "I'm so sorry, I had no idea this would be such a shock."

We paused for a little prayer, and then Eustacia said, "You were telling us what the earlier sisters – the wicked sisters, as we should now call them – did whenever they received a threatening letter from the diocese in the past. What did they do, Hermione?"

"Ignored them, basically." Hermione said. "They put the bad letters in the Bad Things box and just carried on. Raised a bit of money somehow, prayed and kept going."

And, Emelda, as soon as we heard it we realised. Of course! Of course they did. Our predecessors were in far worse straits than us, and they just prayed and kept going. So must we.

Hence the cardboard clock tower. It has a sort of thermometer painted on it. Sister Agnes saw the idea on Blue Peter a little while ago (well, about thirty years). Simple, clever and cheap! I put it into the Shoppe yesterday and already we have £4.32 donated. Nesbitt pointed out that on the scale I had used £4.32 would have to be represented by no more than a hair's breadth of a red line, but she drew it on anyway, so that our fundraising could be underway. We all feel enormously better.

We have risen to the challenge. The fact is that the Diocese cannot give us the money we need to repair the tower, the refectory roof, the drains, the damp or anything else. They simply can't spare it. They have whole cathedrals to prop up and the expense is terrible. Donations are low, even bequests are falling. Whether we're wicked or not, we'll have to manage on our own.

We must follow your example, dear Wanderer; we must use what is to hand and our ingenuity. "Forward ho!" as the girls of Malory Towers would say, or "Trot On!" as Jill would put it.

Best wishes,
Sister B.

15

THE FALL

Dear Traveller,

Late back from confession this evening because of the need to explain to the Almighty, via Father Humbert, about borrowing the community service workers' equipment. Much comforted by Both being of the opinion that it was done in a just cause and that the slight damage to the two hard hats did not amount to anything substantial sin-wise.

All this was because of the refectory roof. The leaks have become so serious that a third of the dining area is unusable and most meals are eaten to the *ping! splash!* of rainwater into buckets. Whilst this is not ideal, it is tolerable, but the recent torrential rain at night has meant that we have had to introduce a rota of sisters who rise at two-hourly intervals and empty the buckets in order to avoid being ankle deep at breakfast.

Since we rise at five for early prayers anyway, this is not popular. But we could bear even the leaks if it were not for the elderly sisters who are inclined to slip and do themselves serious damage when hurrying to table. On Sunday five of them went down like dominos in the dash for scrambled egg. Something had to be done.

Rev Mother, fresh from a workshop entitled "Ecclesiastical Building Repairs: The Hands-on Approach", whose study notes include photographs of veritable cathedrals built by communities (often in California) with absolutely no money or expertise, has decided we should undertake the repairs ourselves. But first we must get up into the roof to inspect it. This fell to Sister Bernard and me. I can't quite remember why, except that I was once on an outward bound course and she was president of her university hang-gliding club.

With such credentials and the Lord behind us, we borrowed ladders, ropes, boiler suits and hard hats from Ted's community service store cupboard and set to. It was locked, but as I explained to Father Humbert, I've always been rather good with locks.

The plan was to haul the ladders up onto the minstrels' gallery and climb from there into the roof space through a trapdoor at one end. The floorboards in the gallery were so rotten that even this was a challenge, but eventually we managed to lean the ladders fairly steadily and recruited Srs Patrick and Matilda, both broad, to hold them.

Up we went, and a terrible height it seemed from up there among the cobwebs, but we squeezed into the roof space and tiptoed along the great timbers to see what might be done. There were three gaping holes in the tiles and several other places where they had shifted. Animal life was thriving. We saw traces of birds, squirrels and possibly rats, and that was without the bat colony, which we discovered when Sister Bernard poked into a corner and about two hundred of them flew straight at us.

To be fair to the bats they meant to fly straight at the hole in the roof, it just happened that we were in the way. Sister Bernard went first, falling, arms flailing, with a crash and cloud of dust, into a heap of damp straw in a corner. Then they swerved and came at me. I remembered, in slow motion, as you do in an emergency, that bats never actually crash into things. Their echo location enables them to swerve just in time. Consoled a little by this I shut my eyes and several of them smacked straight into my face. At this I lurched, put my foot through a timber and sank through the floor up to my armpits.

Shrieks and hysterical prayers could be heard from Patrick and Matilda below. It took an hour to haul me out, dust Sister Bernard down and calm everyone's nerves. The leak is now considerably worse because of the hole I made. It opened up a new course for the roof-stream right onto the middle of the refectory table.

Guiltily returning the equipment to the store, I ran into Ted and had to tell him the whole sad tale. He took it well, wandered off to look at the roof from the outside and returned saying that what we needed was a tarpaulin and he'd see what he could do.

Now I must run to post this before joining the extra prayers for the Lord's safe delivery of your unworthy servant and Sister Bernard. She has one little extra thing to be glad of. Before the bat encounter she planted a TV aerial in the roof space and has hopes of catching the Derby with snow-free reception.

I do hope your day has been less eventful than mine.

Yours, in one piece, by God's blessing,
Sister B.

16

CRIMEWATCH

Dear Pilgrim,

This morning I was laying the last of the swedes into a tempting display outside the Shoppe when I spotted a large man, shaven-headed and scruffily dressed, loitering in the lane. If this had happened yesterday, I would have guessed him to be about to approach and ask for alms, either that or a mendicant friar – they pitch up now and then and are always fed, naturally. But last night, and against my better judgement, I was persuaded to keep the retired sisters company as they watched the new television and happened to see a programme called *Crimewatch UK*.

My dear friend, your calling is too pure for you ever to have heard of such a programme and I urgently recommend you never expose your sensibilities to it, or anything like it. It was an appalling set of reconstructed assaults, murders and building society hold-ups, shown with the purpose of encouraging people who may have witnessed a crime, or have useful information, to contact the police.

The retired sisters watch it, as they explained to me, in the spirit of social responsibility. Who knows how many bank robberies they may stumble across in their daily convent round? It pays to be prepared. I'm sorry to say that last night's programme was full of the tragic stories of young women who went out to nightclubs and then tried to walk home alone only to fall victim to large, shaven-headed men, scruffily dressed, lurking in hedges.

"If only the poor creature had thought to get a mini-cab! She didn't need cash, she could have paid with a credit card!" cried Sister Dymphna, revealing a degree of street-wisdom which took us quite by surprise.

So, this morning, under the influence of *Crimewatch UK*, I found myself wondering whether to lock the till, for which God forgive me. Eventually the stranger came into the Shoppe and declared in a heavy accent, "Sister! Pavel, me. Your roof is broke, yah?" He pointed to the refectory roof, now covered in Ted's welcome tarpaulin, but still definitely "broke".

I said yes, it was, sadly.

"Is bad," observed the man.

I agreed.

He nodded thoughtfully for a while, and then declared, "I fix!"

I then assumed he was a travelling odd-job man of some sort, and explained that we did not have the funds for repairs. This he took a while to understand. When he did, he pointed to his heart and said, "I fix for God. You give food, wood."

And with that he considered the negotiations over and strode off to begin what looked like serious professional surveying.

He was still pacing up and down, jotting notes on a scrap of paper when Rev Mother arrived for her daily visit to the Shoppe. I explained about Pavel and after a short prayer for guidance we decided that he might be an Intervention, so we should give him the benefit of the doubt as long as he remained in full view.

This became more difficult as the morning went on as customers began arriving, all clamouring for potatoes and Hobnobs. But I did my best until I happened to glance up and see Pavel in deep conversation with Sister Carmella. Now, as you know, Sister Carmella is not one for conversation, so this was a surprise. Even more so when she bounded into the Shoppe full of delight and declared him to be a professional Polish builder who had mended ancient roofs all around the Malopolskia region for decades and was eager to help with ours.

By lunchtime Pavel and Carmella had made a list of materials and telephoned it to the building supply company. Apparently they will deliver and let us have thirty days' credit, which proves they never watch *Crimewatch UK*, thank The Lord!

All we need now is to pray for the cash to pay for the materials within the next thirty days. But what are such details to us?

Yours, in eager anticipation of drier dining,
Sister B.

17

THE SWEET BAN

Dear Wanderer in High and Dangerous Places,

Last week I asked Mrs Odge's nephew, who did voluntary service in Peru, what the region you're staying in is like and he told me it is an ideal place for the study of tropical diseases because the mosquitos and the humidity combine in a particularly propitious way – but only for the mosquitos. "An absolute armpit!" was his summary of the living conditions for humans.

I do hope you are well and that the exercise books we sent have arrived. I tucked one or two rulers and pencils in too to keep you going, and there may even be a newspaper. I know you enjoy a Review Section, even one that is three months out of date. Enjoy!

I write in the quiet of a Thursday night when nearly all the sisters have gone to Billericay for the Bridgettines' special benediction and bread and cheese supper. Angelina and Merce are here, because it's National Science Week and they are demonstrating their telescope to a group from the Village College. Rain is no problem, apparently.

I opted to stay because I need to make one or two rearrangements in the Shoppe after last night's convocation. After discussion we agreed that it was wrong to sell sweets to the schoolchildren, even if it is also very profitable. Their teeth will be damaged and they will get a terrible thing which is all in letters – ATCP or something – which is a bad form of what used to be called the fidgets, because of all the sugar and colourings.

I know this is right. I absolutely bow to the general decision, but I can't help wondering as I box up the Hula Hoops and the Wispas, what the young customers will say when they arrive tomorrow and find them gone. Crisps are still on the menu, but only healthy parsnip and beetroot ones, which the children abominate, and all the fizzy drinks are going back to Hedgeby's too.

What with our commitment to a neutral carbon footprint and our policy of not selling products which may in any way lead our customers away from the straight and narrow path, we have ended up with an unusual range of goods, to say the least. Our drinks, for example, now consist only of a wholefood mango and apricot juice, a brand of organic apple concentrate that comes from Belgium, and Sacre Coeur Spring Water whose unique selling point is that it is bottled at source by praying nuns in Shropshire (and at £1.99 a bottle, you'd hope they were very virtuous nuns, too). It all seems a bit *recherché* and not the simple, useful and rather homely stock I had pictured at the beginning of the venture.

Nesbitt will be in for a shock, as the sweets were her idea. I'm not sure how she'll take it. I am afraid of losing lots of customers, my assistant and all our profits. Then how are we to pay for roof linings or have the minibus repaired? This is defeatist, I know, but I am beginning to think the Shoppe may not be enough to generate the funds we need. Or perhaps it is I, the Shoppe-keeper who is to blame. Perhaps I am just no good at the retail business – I certainly underestimated its complexities.

I mentioned this at convocation last week and now rather regret having done so because the message passed back to the retired sisters was that the Shoppe was failing and it was all hands to the pumps. The dear sisters rallied round and came up with the idea of handmade gifts, which they are sure will sell at huge prices, be irresistible to the public and drag the Shoppe (if not the nation) out of its recession before you can say pipe-cleaner priests.

It is actually little priest figures made of pipe-cleaners and dressed in tiny black surplices that are their big idea, although pegs dressed as nuns and embroidered bookmarks also feature. It's a long time since she made one, but Mother Hilda thinks a hair picture might fetch a good price too. Perhaps luckily, Hermione has short hair, which would be no good at all for a picture. Frankly, I'm relieved. There used to be dozens of hair pictures made from the hair cut from novices when they took their vows hanging in the long hall, and it would be fair to say that they weren't to everyone's taste.

Anyway, all day long, elderly sisters have been arriving in the Shoppe with armfuls of their creations. Emelda, I do not doubt the care or the skill with which they are made, or even their charm, it's just that I can't see how they fit in with the things we sell in the Shoppe. Eventually Nesbitt and I cleared off a high shelf right at the back and put them up there. Nesbitt rather likes the pipe-cleaner priests and has taken to moving little outcrops of them around; one day by the cabbages, one day near the dog biscuits. Nobody's bought one yet, though.

On reflection I feel nothing but shame for mentioning such trivialities to you, whose trials are far greater. We never get crocodiles here and generally the weather, while grey and a bit bleak sometimes, is reasonably welcoming to humans. Where you are it seems to be hostile in every way, yet you have never complained. You are a great inspiration and I wish there was more to cheer you in this letter. Please remember your friends at St Winifreda's in your prayers, and we will do the same for you and your lovely schoolchildren.

Oh, and Sister Annunziata says do not bathe in the standing water, and don't eat the grey parts of the Deoduerte fish.

Best wishes,
Sister B

18

PRIMARY SCHOOL TRIP

Dear Fearless Traveller in the Lord's work,

Father Humbert has tonsillitis again, so Sr Agnes had to do his prison visit. The result is that I have done a little travelling myself, standing in for her on a coach trip with the primary reception class to Hunstanton. Small beer to those such as yourself who ford torrents and chop a daily thirty mile path through rainforests perhaps, but pretty eventful all the same.

On the coach, Mrs Pettigrew, the class teacher, directed me towards a solemn little boy, handing me a carrier bag as she did so and saying, "Arthur is usually sick on bus journeys. You won't mind sitting with him, will you?" I wondered what the bag could contain (shower cap and oilskins?), but dare not look in case it offended the poor lad.

"Hello," he said wanly. "I'm called Arthur. I'm usually sick on bus journeys."

As we pulled away, a rosy-cheeked girl with corkscrew curls popped her head over the back of the seat in front and piped up, "That's Arthur, he's my friend. He's usually sick on bus journeys." Nobody could say I wasn't warned.

Conversation with excited five and six-year-olds is anarchic but very entertaining. They begin by offering random pieces of information about themselves: "I can't do shoelaces, my fingers go all twisty" or "My brother's got a snake!" and then all hearers pitch in with a comment or their own piece of information – which needn't be connected in any way.

This continues until someone says something that makes everyone giggle so much they fall over. Since almost everything makes people of five or six giggle, even the solemn ones like Arthur, conversation needn't go on for very long. Top marks, of course, go to anyone who can mention "poo" or "wee", but they were on their best behaviour around me and only whispered it in a very tickly way into each others' ears.

We ate our sandwiches at half past ten, as you do on coach trips, and were there before we'd played even half of Mrs Pettigrew's planned pen-and-paper games. Inside the aquarium the children strode straight past most exhibits, but were hypnotised by anything that was either huge or very ugly or could strip a body to the bare bones in seconds.

My own favourite were the Cow Fish. These are the only square fish in nature. There must be sense to it – perhaps their particular part of the coral reef is cubist – but the shape is no good at all, really, for directional swimming. Their rather inadequate fins are positioned along the bottom edge of their square little bodies, but no matter how hard they beat and swirl them about they only ever seem to go vaguely in the direction they'd intended, and end up bobbing in a very comical way. Oh, and they're bright yellow and have two little horns. It makes you wonder what the Almighty was about, but He obviously had His reasons.

Once we had prevented the bouncier children from throwing themselves or each other into the tank with the rays, and retrieved all the dawdlers, it was time for the souvenir shop before we had an hour on the beach. Agonies of indecision over which pencil to buy for which brother or sister and which balloon for themselves were all forgotten in the stampede down to the sea. They frolicked, skimmed stones, paddled, wrote in the sand, dug trenches, built castles and generally did what all children do on a beach with all their might until it was time for an ice cream (Mrs Pettigrew's treat) and the bus home.

The rain held off, the wind wasn't too sharp, there were oystercatchers and coloured pebbles and waves and the taste of salt on the breeze. And even poor Arthur slept all the way home. What a treat!

In grateful praise for all His Creation, especially the seaside, Arthur and his friends, and cowfish.

Best wishes,
Sister B

19

Free Samples

Dear Brave Scaler of the Rio Fuerte cliffs,

Is that you, the dot hanging by its fingertips over 1,000 feet of thin air? It looks terribly dangerous, but the views are astonishing. Thank you for the photographs, which are now attracting awe and admiration in the Shoppe.

"You wouldn't catch me up there!" was Mrs Odge's rather practical response. Since she's a well-upholstered lady in her fifties with no climbing ambitions, I guess she's right, but for some reason the remark gave Nesbitt a terrible fit of the giggles. She had to pretend to do things in the cold store.

Along with your letter this morning came one from Ira and Nancy Marciano of Tampa, Florida, who are planning a vacation soon in the area and wondered whether we offered accommodation. However did they discover us, I wonder?

"Americans! How exciting!" said Rev Mother when I showed her the letter. "Write and say our guest accommodation will be ready soon. Guest rooms are on the list for this year, so it will only be a small leap of faith." She's unstoppable.

I mentioned the mystery of the Americans to Hermione and she said, "Oh, that must be the website. Alphonsus is piloting it and he put some information about us online. They must have read it. I've been giving him the early history of the Order to put on as I go through the papers. It's only a first draft, really, but why keep it to ourselves? It's really interesting. Most of the sisters came from London originally. They wanted the quietest and most inaccessible place in East Anglia and Hog Fen was it."

This week I went to a do-it-yourself superstore for the first time. Carmella needed potting compost and I pass the place on the way back from outpatients, so I thought it would save time. What a mistake. For one thing it was gigantic and Mother Maria Celeste and I couldn't work out where anything was. Then we needed a trolley and didn't have one, then when we did find one it had a lock and you needed a coin and we didn't have one of those either. The whole experience was just making us feel incompetent and sad when we heard birdsong. We looked up into the steel rafters of the lofty place, and wondered if they were piping it through loudspeakers, but then Maria spotted a robin, a real, live robin, sitting on a display of plant pots and singing. It was filling the giant hangar with its sharp little song. Everyone who saw it smiled and stopped.

Someone helped us with the trolley and we succeeded in buying the compost and making our escape. Unless they always have a robin in full song,

I don't plan to return, but I'm glad we saw it. I hope it found its way out more easily than we did.

Nesbitt is bagging dog biscuits as I write this. I have discovered something very surprising about her. Although she is naturally shy, and inclined to be monosyllabic, she is a wonderful natural sales-woman. I tend to assume people don't really want or need things, and would be better off keeping their money; Nesbitt does not. Yesterday she persuaded Mrs Odge – Mrs Odge! – to try Convent Ginger Shortbread. Free samples. She cut it into tiny pieces and offered them on a plate. Delphine Odge, who probably hasn't tried anything new since 1973, bought four boxes. That's over £6 on biscuits!

Hedgeby saw it and said, "I'd hang on to that girl, she's got something."

I must close now and help put out the biscuit sam-ples for Dr Greengross and his team. They visit once a year and take blood samples from us all, but their par-ticular favourites are Merce and Angelina. It's long-term research; this is their thirty-seventh year. They especially like us because we stay put and tend not to do the things other people do to damage their health. This year they've agreed to act as volunteers for us in return by sampling and scoring our biscuits.

Dr Greengross had no hesitation; "I have eight post-graduates and two nurses in my team and none of them has ever refused a biscuit," he said. "They are connoisseurs! I can promise you the keenest focus group and the finest feedback. Just make sure you lay in plenty of stocks!"

We'll do the tasting after the Ceremony of the Socks – Angelina and Merce have a tradition of knitting a pair of socks (one each) for Dr Greengross every year. The socks used to be plain thirty years ago, but they are expert knitters as well as mathematicians, so over the years they have developed patterns of the most extraordinary complexity to challenge each other and delight the doctor.

Last year the sock theme was the double helix, with patterns representing the structures of DNA. Sometimes the socks contain riddle patterns or knitted mathematical puzzles, so Dr G has a year to solve them and announces his answer just before the next pair is presented. Every year he pretends to get the answer wrong, claims the puzzle was inhumanly difficult and has defeated not only him but his team, and all his Nobel prize-winning colleagues. And then (of course) he gets it right. It's quite an occasion.

We have five varieties of biscuit for the tasters: Armadillos, Llamas, St Winnies, Guinea Pigs and Sisterbreads. Early testing shows Shoppe customers favour Guinea Pigs (crisp cinnamon semi-circles) by a slight margin, with Sisterbreads (shaped short-breads) close behind. Of course, it's consumer research and not a competition, but the various bakers are taking a very close interest in the results, and I rather hope it isn't my job to announce them.

Best wishes,
Sister B.

20

CAR PARKING

Dear Toiler in the Vinyards of Far Off Lands,

Iwrite this to the jolly sound of whistling and hammering; Pavel has already begun on the timbers for the refectory roof. He works very hard for long hours, singing merrily in Polish all the while. He wears a hard hat, lent to him unofficially by Ted from the community service stores, but only, I think, to humour us. All he asks in return is food.

Since this is all he asks, and since we are so grateful, we have had to put our heads together to work out how best to feed him. We had forgotten how very much hungry workmen eat! Nesbitt to the rescue! I only had to say, "Oh dear, I can't imagine what we can give Pavel…" and she sprang into action.

"What can we spare?" she asked, looking around the stock cupboard. "What's cheap and easy? I know: sandwiches! I can make sandwiches. I've got four brothers and I do all the packed lunches. We'll do sandwiches for his tea breaks and lunch and maybe we could spare him a cake for later. Can I use some of these eggs? And can we get a kettle so I can make him some tea?"

So with a bit of re-arrangement we cleared a workspace for her in the back room and she began producing piles of sandwiches and cups of tea. She carries them out several times a day in an old apple box she found somewhere and Pavel is delighted. If there are any left over, I wrap them and they are already quite popular with the office workers and even the schoolchildren, who still come, despite the sweet ban.

The only little worry we still had was how to raise the money to pay the builders' merchants. As I watched from below I was painfully aware that every plank and every nail and tile was "on tick", as they used to say.

We had already held special prayers and a dedicated intercession to try to help raise the money when Mr Hedgeby happened into the Shoppe with his latest samples, Fructis shampoo and Fruit Corners.

A smartly suited man strode past him and presented himself to me as "Roger Collis, CEO, Intermediax".

I was confused and wondered whether this was a job title I should understand, when Mr Hedgeby said, "Oh yes, that'd be that company over on Odge's Lodge, as was."

"I need to talk to your site manager about parking," said Mr Collis.

I hesitated so long that Mr Hedgeby swung into action.

"I advise the sisters on that sort of thing." he declared.

"Well," said Roger Collis, "we at Intermediax have the East Anglian launch of our new product, ACTCM, next Thursday and I was wondering whether we might come to some sort of accommodation over car parking."

I was about to say yes of course we could, when Mr Hedgeby gave me a signal I couldn't quite fathom with his eyebrow.

"That would depend…" he replied, inscrutably.

"Naturally we would pay the going rate. We need about twenty spaces and there's ample room on your verge opposite, but I thought I'd better check with you. In case you had plans."

"What would you call the going rate then?" asked Hedgeby, as casually as he could manage.

"Oh, I don't know – how about ten pounds per car for the day?"

I gave the game away slightly by gasping. £200 for allowing cars we can't even see to use a strip of land none of us had even remembered!

"I shall have to put it to the Reverend Mother, of course…and it may take some time," said Hedgeby. "And of course there may be damage…"

"Perhaps if I paid cash in advance it would be easier?" asked our neighbour the tycoon, peeling notes from a bundle as he spoke.

In two minutes Mr Hedgeby, whose Fructis I have even now displayed in a very prominent position, had garnered from Mr Collis enough to pay for the repairs to the refectory roof. And what is more both were satisfied with the transaction.

God bless ACTCM by Intermediax! Only He knows what it is.

Best wishes,
Sister B.

2 1

UNDERWEAR

Dear Wanderer,

Have you ever heard of a company called Damart? I doubt you have, since your mission has largely taken you to warmer climates. Exposed as we are in these parts to the coldest of east winds, the name is as sweet music to our chilblained ears. These kind people provide underclothes cunningly made using the latest technology. The space age comes into it somewhere; I believe they use Teflon. Or is that frying pans?

Anyway, light and durable garments can be had from Damart which, worn under the habit, enable the wearer to stride forth into garden or Shoppe oblivious of even the fiercest of wind-chill factors. And what an effect this has on the spirits! Without her thermal underwear, Sister Carmella is frankly a different woman in winter and one you wouldn't want to meet without a short prayer, I'm afraid.

We never admire the stoutness of spirit of the generations of sisters who have built and lived at St

Winifreda's so much as when we wonder why it never occurred to any of them to build fireplaces in most of the obvious places. Did they not suffer from cold feet? Or did they consider that purple extremities, numb and painful, were inevitable in the religious life?

The retired sisters often tell us we are getting softer. Mother Hilda remarked yesterday that she had never seen a radiator until she was in her twenties when she gave herself a nasty burn on one in a Lyons Corner House during the blackout. To hear her talk one would assume that earlier generations were simply warmed from the inside by a special old-fashioned holiness. Perhaps she is right, though it must be pointed out that she pronounced these views with her chair pressed to one of the radiators in the retired nuns' quarters, which represent the only central heating the convent has.

The reason for all this harping on cold and underwear is that it falls to the Shoppe to raise the money for what Rev Mother calls the Underwear Renewal Fund. For some reason last year was a particularly hard one in terms of thermal underwear deterioration. Many garments fell to shreds through hard wear, despite Mother Mathilda's extraordinary skill at repairs.

Grumbles were heard about the lack of durability of clothing these days – until, that is, we looked up in the purchase book to see when the last set was bought and found it was 1981. Three decades isn't a bad innings for a pair of Long Johns or a vest, so we stopped complaining and dedicated a convocation to new ideas for funding replacements. None emerged. So by default, as the profit-making arm of the convent (as Rev Mother rather intimidatingly puts it), the fundraising falls to the Shoppe.

Sadly I had to reject the only suggestion so far, which came from Nesbitt. She thought another thermometer-style chart in the Shoppe might attract donations – depicting giant thermal Long Johns perhaps? Naughty Nesbitt. Mr Hedgeby turned quite pale.

All prayers and marketing strategies welcome.

Best wishes,
Sister B.

22

RATS AND PUMPKINS

Dear Builder for the Lord,

How we enjoyed your letter! Your resourcefulness at Santo Domingo is amazing – a whole new school building from nothing but mud, dung and a few branches. Mud is something we have a very bountiful supply of here in Three Fens, and there are a few branches lying around just waiting to be put to use since Sister Carmella commissioned her new chainsaw. We only have dung from the chickens ourselves, but Farmer Odge next door has eight hundred pigs, so I'm sure he'd let us have a little from there.

All we need is a few volunteers and we could knock up a buttress for the bell tower in no time. If only things were so simple. Instead we have the buildings inspector coming with a parish councillor tomorrow to examine our roof repairs, we are all a little nervous of these representatives of a higher authority, although of course our own Higher Authority always gets us through.

I was collecting the post from the old bell tower yesterday morning – which involves standing on a little stool and plunging my arm into the arrow slit on one side of the door – when a large whiskery man (I took him to be a rambler) stopped to admire it.

"Fine old thing," he said. "Lovely bit of neo-gothic. Unrivalled, I'd say, in East Anglia."

I said yes, we were very fond of our tower, but a little worried by its upkeep.

"Are you losing gargoyles and decorative stonework?"

"We are," I said. "It's getting serious. You can see the cracks from here."

"Are you members of the FTPS?" he asked.

"The what?"

"The Folly Towers Preservation Society. I am. I love the things. I trek all round the country seeking them out. Lots of people do. If you joined, the tower would go into the guidebook. It helps with raising money."

"You'd probably have to pay to join," I said. "We haven't the funds."

"Well, listen," he said. "I'm the president, actually. We could certainly make a reduction for religious communities, and it really is a lovely example of its kind. It deserves to be preserved."

He took out his camera. "Could you run to fifteen pounds, say?"

"We do have fourteen pounds twenty-six in the fundraising collection, as a matter of fact."

"Well then, welcome to the Folly Towers Association. I'm Philip Downs. I'll put these pictures on the website and you can expect a few more visitors. Do you keep it locked?"

"Yes, it's not safe. We still use the bell, but only occasionally."

"Oh, the bell's intact," he said, interested.

"Yes, but the stairs are wooden and quite rickety."

"Would you consider opening it up for members to visit? By prior arrangement, obviously. A small charge, say five pounds a head would be the usual thing, and it would bring you a few more customers for the Shoppe."

So the deal was done. I took Mr Downs over to Rev Mother's office, and he has already added the Folly Tower of St Winifreda-in-the-Fen to the website. Alphonsus showed it to us on his tiny little phone and very fine it looked. You can hardly see the giant cracks at all.

Meanwhile there is a little difficulty you can perhaps advise on. I'm afraid we have rats. Every year the autumn brings them off the fields in search of a nice dry winter hiding place and an awful lot of them head for the convent. I know they are all God's creatures, but they make so much noise in the rafters that it keeps us all awake, and last year they nibbled one of the electricity cables and cut off the supply to the dormitories.

We managed well enough with candles, many sisters in fact preferred them, but Pavel was appalled and said, "No, Sister! Is fire coming! Is very bad! Very Bad!"

We prayed over the question at convocation all last week, and so far the favoured solution is a visit from the pest controller. But that costs £70 – a terrible sum and way beyond the budget, so we'll just have to pray some more. What do you do about rats in South America? Are they a problem? Not to sisters of your calibre, I imagine.

The Shoppe is doing quite well at the moment. The sale of giant pumpkins has pushed takings up. I couldn't help noticing that Parson's Farm, just down the road, sell them at astonishingly inflated prices, so I marked ours up a little, feeling like Sainsbury's reacting to a slightly underhand Tesco initiative.

Sister Carmella and her community service team have produced a bumper crop, and many of great size, so I piled them up at the entrance gate to draw the crowds in. This is called a "teaser" and is recommended by Mr Menon. Several local families bought one for each child and the Cottenhams took a dozen for a party, so I was cheerfully totting up the bounty when Sister Mary of Light rushed in and said, "Do you know, Sister, those pumpkins might be being used for devil worship?"

I wasn't quite sure what she was talking about. I thought the pumpkins were used for soup – they make very good and very economical soup, as I'm sure you know. I have seen some carved into lanterns outside people's homes as I deliver veg, but I was certainly not aware that this amounted to anything like worship of the Evil One. The Shoppe's piled pumpkins looked entirely innocent to me.

But of course it would be the more innocent vegetable that Satan would go for, as Sr Mary pointed out. So I sold no more pumpkins that day, and at convocation we discussed the issue: Pumpkins; do they invite sin? We're still awaiting guidance on that one, but a useful compromise was proposed by Rev Mother, which was to re-label the stock Delicious Soup Squash, so as to discourage devilish practices. She also pointed out that while the wider issue certainly needs consideration, the immediate one is over as it is already October 31st.

I wonder whether a few suitably carved soup squash might deter rats. Perhaps if I carve them with a skull and crossbones or a profile of Mr Wooler the financial adviser. (God forgive me – GFM – as the Benedictine sisters in New Jersey put it in their emails.) What do you think?

Blessings and good wishes to you all, and our parcel of pens for the new classroom is on its way,
Sister B.

23
A RAT SMELT

Dear Sister Emelda,

What a day! I was grateful for the delightful distraction of your letter. The retreat centre in the mountains sounds delightful! Imagine peace all day and beautiful hilly surroundings – heaven! Here on the flat we have had a heat-wave for the last week or so. It's brought out a lot of flowers and even a few late vegetables, it's even encouraged ramblers along the footpath and into the Shoppe for refreshment, so I've been busy selling them hearty slabs of Lemon Drizzle cake and Elderflower Cordial – handmade by Nesbitt to recipes by a cook with a very long name (Hugh something double-barrelled: Friendly-Withenshaw?). Sister Bernard found one of his books in a skip. Hugh's cakes are just the solid stick-to-the-ribs type of cake favoured by ramblers, so we're doing rather well.

One woman walker, weighed down with carrot cake, admired the decor in the Shoppe and wanted to photograph some of the enamel pails and jugs on the windowsill. They are shabby chic, apparently!

She was not tempted to photograph the minibus, which is entirely shabby and lacking all chic. Not only is it losing small bits almost every week now – last week the ignition key got stuck and yesterday a window handle fell off – but it's also developed a dreadful smell. I hardly dared mention it to the passengers who had enough to worry about with their visit to the dentist, but it grew steadily stronger as the drive wore on. I fear the expense of taking it to the garage, but what else can I do? I can't transport vegetables in something that smells as if something is rotting inside it. It'll get into the cauliflowers.

Oh dear, I do hope this note full of troubles and trivialities will not disrupt your tranquil contemplations. Pray for us – and the minibus.

Love and best wishes,
Sister B.

24
CALL ME BOB

Dear Sister Emelda,

We all very much appreciated your helpful advice on the rat problem. A pack of feral dogs seems a wonderfully cheap and effective solution, if only there were such a thing in Three Fens. There are a few dogs about, naturally, but Lady Cottenham and Farmer Odge keep rather superior animals. Monty, Lady Cottenham's Labradoodle (no, honestly, that's what they're called) is too bouncy and good-natured, I think, for serious ratting. Hodge's assorted terriers would certainly know what to do with a rat, but he keeps them busy over at his place. They follow him everywhere and respond instantly to any gruff command – it's rather impressive. I fear they wouldn't behave quite the same way if someone else gave them orders.

Certainly the chickens ignore my authority. We had a little incident last week when two of the sillier hens got on the wrong side of the fence and Jean-Paul, the cockerel, became frantic to bring them back into his fold and bashed his head on the fence post. There was blood and we feared a trip to the vet, but Sister Carmella and I managed to grab him – she has an impressive sprint speed for a woman in her seventies – and in the end I just used Germolene and a plaster. He looks a little less stylish than usual, but the hens don't seem to mind.

The balmy weather continues here and brings the great bonus of hungry country walkers eager to buy refreshments in the Shoppe. Their numbers have been increased by the Folly Tower visitors – a particularly jolly and hungry lot, who arrive by the coachload. They pay £5 to look all around and inside the tower and then spend the same again on cake and still insist on handing over generous donations to the tower fund. Nesbitt can hardly keep up with the rising line on the cardboard tower.

The power of cake is a revelation. We've only offered homemade cakes for a few weeks. It started with Nesbitt baking for the Polish roofer, but it's a good source of profit, especially now that Sister Clementine has joined us. A genuine French cook!

Of course, we sisters allow ourselves very few meals that could possibly put her talents to good use, but customers' eyes light up whenever they spot one of her amazing *patisseries*. The only adaptation she has had to make is to re-size her delicate little gateaux for the East Anglian market; tripling them, approximately. I'm often astonished when I am serving in the Shoppe at how quickly people pick up the scent of one of Sister Clementine's deliveries. It's at least half a mile from here to the nearest desk in the Smithy Fen business units, but a hungry office worker can be at the door inside three minutes.

Pavel is particularly partial to Clementine's éclairs, and we like to give him first pick. This morning he polished off half a dozen of them between mending the guttering over the front porch and fixing up the Shoppe's latest improvement – a community notice board. One side of this is for free notices, which are of interest to the villagers and other Shoppe customers, and the other side is for little paid advertisements.

It took a lot of discussion before agreement could be reached over this at convocation. We want to steer well clear of any Murdoch-like tendency to sell advertising and control the village's media, but on the other hand a noticeboard seemed quite handy, and people are always asking me to put up cards or posters, so why not ask for a little contribution? (Are these precisely the thoughts that led to News International's foundation, I wonder?)

This whole idea came from someone called Bob Fairbrother ("Hello, I'm Bob Fairbrother!") who introduced himself as a new neighbour from the business park last week. Mr Fairbrother ("Do call me Bob!") is, according to his card, an "Inspirational Speaker and Business Trainer – Inventor of Fairbrother's Five Steps to Better Marketing". Bob is now the Shoppe's marketing adviser – self-appointed, but welcome all the same. He thinks we should make more of the retired sisters' "Handmade

Gifts" shelf. "Loads of potential in religious knick-knacks, Sister. You'd be amazed."

On his first visit to the Shoppe he bought four whole coffee and walnut cakes for delegates to his latest conference – an extraordinary extravagance which doubled the day's takings at a stroke, but also left the cake shelves rather empty. Poor Pavel's face fell when he popped in at teatime. "Ah, Sister, is nothing left for me?" All Nesbitt's sandwiches had long been sold. I offered him beetroot crisps, but it wasn't the same.

I must find something I can hold in reserve and bring out when all the cakes have gone. Ah well, that's one for prayers and convocation, but not tonight because we have tai chi! Rev Mother has decided that our fitness is very important, and after much research she has found a teacher willing to run a weekly class in return for a box of vegetables and our grateful thanks. How exciting!

Good luck with the school sports!

Best wishes,
Sister B.

25

THE NEW DENTIST AND EMBARRASSING BODIES

Dear Sister Emelda,

How is the weather in Santo Domingo? Here it is mild and dry, the wind only occasionally sharp. We have a glut of apples and have stored a great many, but we have also been experimenting with drying them, and yesterday Sister Clementine made a batch of Apple and Sage Jelly, which smelled quite delicious, and which has sold remarkably quickly.

Sister Gertrude, who was working alongside, tried an experiment which was something called Apple Leather, where you reduce the apple pulp by baking it for a very long time into a fruity biltong or jerky. Very useful for putting into your saddlebags on a long day's ride – I've parcelled some up for you. Watch your teeth!

Teeth are a bit of a problem here at the moment. Rats' teeth are gnawing all around us. We worry about the wiring, and if they got into the Shoppe it would be very serious. Nuns' teeth are also making us pray for guidance because our old dentist recently retired. He had always charged us the fixed rate of £5 per visit, and we thought that was the going NHS rate. What a fair and decent system this is, we told ourselves over the years. But then Mr Ingold took retirement and was replaced by Martina Carter-Fielding, a brisk young woman who wears a suit and high heels under her plastic apron.

After she had treated two elderly sisters last week she gave me a card and said, "Just take that to Susan at reception, and she'll sort out the next appointment and the fees."

Susan is new too. She looked at the card and tapped on her computer and then she said, "That will be £326.78, please. Will you pay now or at the end of the treatments?"

I would have fallen over with shock, but I was supporting Mother Matilda Rey on one side and Sister Patrick on the other, and nobody wants to see a row of nuns go over like skittles in a public place. Discussions ensued and it emerged, of course, that Mr Ingold, dear man, had never charged us anything like the going rate. What we will do now is in the hands of the Almighty, so that means we don't need to worry, but we do need to pray because we have a lot of teeth between us. How are such things arranged in South America? Somehow I imagine lovely devout dentists willing to treat in return for nothing more than a benediction available on every side, but it may be that I am behind the times.

I will have to end soon because I am on television duty this evening, which means popping over to the Father Edward Wilson Centre and turning the set on at 6 pm. I have to read the television programme in the newspaper first and decide which channels to select for the evening ahead until lights out at 9.30 pm. It's quite a responsibility because the sisters over at the Centre may be a little weak in body, but they are certainly strong on punctuality and critical opinion – as well they might be after lives spent fearlessly serving the Lord in war zones, inner cities or contemplative cells here and abroad. Woe betide the TV monitor who arrives late and goes for Channel 4 when *Autumnwatch* or anything with David Attenborough is on BBC 2!

All this monitoring is the result of the terrible *Embarrassing Bodies* fiasco a few weeks ago. We are not really very used to the television yet, and at one time we just turned it on in the Centre sitting room and left the sisters to enjoy whatever it showed. But I was cleaning the parquet floor in the connecting passageway with Sister Agnes that evening, when we heard what sounded like a murderous attack taking place. We ran towards the sound of shrieks and prayers, dreading what we would find, but it turned out to be their reaction to a particularly embarrassing body!

Now many of these women, as you know, have been nurses – and front line ones too – but whatever it was they saw left them so traumatised that none of them touched the shortbread biscuits and several vowed there and then never to watch television again.

The result is the TV monitoring rota, which is designed to avoid exposing the over-nineties to anything Embarrassing. But of course, they like a bit of stimulation too, so all wildlife programmes are fine, except that recent one where they filmed a hippo corpse over several nights as it was eaten by practically every slavering animal and bird in Africa. That one, I'm afraid, had me praying to forget the tiny moment of it I accidentally glimpsed. The poor dead creature was blown up like a jolly inflatable at first glance, but when you looked again you realised its limbs were sticking out in rigor mortis as vultures ripped shreds off its face.

"Jesus, Mary and Joseph," as Eustacia put it, "what in God's name will they think of next?"

That is a truly terrible image to leave you with, my dear sister, so I will add something far more cheerful. Sister Patrick has surrounded the gardens with the most beautifully carved pumpkins. She lights them each evening as part of her programme to overcome the negativity of Halloween. Each one is carved with a little reference to the Bible, so there are angels, stars, fish and even what might be a whale (but definitely no dead hippos) twinkling away all down the drive. Pavel was very impressed.

Blessings to you all,
Sister B.

26

THE DISAGREEABLE TRAIN LADY

Dear Traveller,

A beautiful clear day here. Leaves turning on the hedges and a mild sun. We have tiny crocuses under the Scots Pine. And yet how far from my bad-tempered mind such peaceful pleasures have been. Apologies, Emelda, if I use this note as a confessional, but I have to get it off my chest and Father Humbert won't be here until Easter now – he came off his bicycle on the way to the Samaritans.

I was sitting on the train this afternoon on my way back from visiting Mother Hilda in hospital (nothing serious) and I was settling down nicely to enjoy the country views for a few moments when on bustled a lady in her sixties with a mild-faced dog. Now, Emelda, you'll know as well as I do that there are some people who take positive action to avoid anyone in religious dress on a train, and there are some people who are drawn to them like a magnet. It's an occupational hazard.

Well, this lady plonks down beside me, even though there were twenty free seats on the carriage, then opens the local paper and reads aloud a headline saying, "Six hundred new homes for Three Fens – plans approved".

"Well!" she says aloud. "That's not going to make people very happy in Three Fens. Nobody wants six hundred houses on their doorstep! Why do they do it? And such horrible houses too! Nobody wants to buy those cramped little places. No garden. It'll all be foreigners. Poles, probably! What is the country coming to? Honestly, they'd never do this sort of thing in France, or in Germany, and the Americans don't go building little boxes everywhere!"

On and on she went. She hardly drew breath. She swiftly condemned gypsies, all Eastern Europeans, all Indians and everyone from Africa in similar terms. They come over here and fill up the housing stock. They work for less than the minimum wage and take jobs from local people, they take benefits and have huge families. They're all the same.

"My husband worked on the Olympic Velodrome, you know," she brayed. "He's an architect – you wouldn't believe the tricks these people get up to."

I was outraged. She was wrong on every count. We have Eastern European sisters in the convent, we have Indians and Africans too. And what about my dear customers and students? How could I sit by and hear her condemn people like Pavel? He has worked wonders for no payment and been jolly while he did it. No Emelda, I couldn't leave this unchallenged. I just couldn't! She had to be confronted.

I was actually opening my mouth to say something when my eye fell on a note stuck to the book she was holding. Written on it in large letters were two words: "MIND YOURSELF".

This stopped me in my tracks. What could it mean? Was it something she had written? Had someone else written it and left it there as a warning? A threat, even? Had the doctor recommended Post-its to help her get a grip?

I'll never know. The moment had gone. We were at Fen Water and I could only climb out without having stood up to her in any way. Everyone in the carriage would have assumed that I absolutely agreed – that the Church absolutely agreed, for all I know. What a shame! I feel a coward. I will offer it up; that's all I can think of.

Perhaps Rev Mother can find me a course – Speaking Up in Public – that's the sort of title it needs. Although they usually have an exclamation mark these days, I've noticed, so it'll probably be Answering Back for GOOD!

Pray for my patience!

Best wishes,
Sister B.

27

SUBMISSION

Dear Emelda,

How absolutely right you were in your reply. Of course it is our duty to speak up – speak out – stand up for ourselves (select your preferred phrasal verb) and others as loudly and promptly as we can at all times. It's just that some of us are more naturally equipped to do so than others. I have had a lot of advice since.

Summed up, it comes to this. Either 1) Get in fast. As soon as you begin to be irritated by someone in a public place, say loudly, "I think you are wrong!", "I do not agree!", "That is not an opinion I share!", "Speak for yourself!" etc. and keep saying it until they, and all who are listening, hear very clearly. Or – and this is the other school of thought – 2) Say nothing. Assertiveness in public argument has very little place in the religious life. We need to be as unassertive as possible. This is not to say that we agree cravenly with whatever opinions are being sounded off, certainly not, but our mission is not to concern ourselves with what other people think; we should humbly accept that everyone is entitled to their own view EVEN IF THEY ARE COMPLETELY WRONG. It's called submission.

So here I am, stuck in the mire between Assertion on the one hand – a virtue I imagine to look very like the French Revolution's Marianne, bare-shouldered and muscular – and Submission, a shambling figure, who never makes eye-contact. Ah well, I pray and keep praying...

Best wishes,
Sister B.

28

SUPERMODELS

Dear Sister Emelda,

Thank you so much for the chili flakes and cumin. They were a little late to arrive because they had to be opened and tested by HM Customs. Apparently their sniffer dogs went crazy. They must have forgotten to put them back in the post for a couple of months, but they're here now and enlivening our pumpkin soups considerably.

It's very quiet at St Winifreda's today because most of the sisterhood has gone to the Benedictine's conference at Littleport: "Forward in Faith in the Fens". It's a big do, with a tented service, a prayer parade and a feast, so they'll all be having a high old time. The sharp easterly wind will only enliven their enjoyment – we're used to that sort of thing; the Poor Claires will feel it because they're used to the balmy south coast, but they're easily holy enough to avoid distraction.

It was my turn to be on duty here, so I waved them off at 8 am and now I'm taking a few moments

out from decorating a Saint's Day cake for Rev
Mother. I have just wrapped her present, which is a
tiny little thing you plug into a slot in the side of a
computer and use for photographs somehow. Don't
ask me any of the technicalities. It's so small that I
dropped it earlier and had a lot of difficulty finding it under the refectory table, but it's capable of
storing something like 10,000 photographs. I only
needed a piece of paper two inches square to wrap
it, but in the end I decided to put it into a shoebox:
more of a surprise!

After that I shall double-check the minibus. I
might have mentioned it before. Its age is against it,
I'm afraid, and now it leaks oil, but at least it doesn't
smell any more thanks to the cleaning team at the
supermarket.

Do you know they have teams of people in the car
parks of supermarkets these days who will very oblig-
ingly clean your car while you are shopping? They
are usually, in these parts anyway, Lithuanian. They
absolutely refuse to take money from nuns, so usually I give them a veg box. This time, when I opened
the minibus to reach it, the cleaning team – a strap-
ping half-dozen uniformed Lithuanian supermodels
of both genders, reeled back as the smell hit them.

"Wow! What is smell?" asked their leader,
Marlene Dietrich in a boiler suit.

I said I didn't know what it was or what to do
about it.

"You want we check? Is very serious this smell!
We check. Come!" And she summoned the team,

some of whom dived inside the minibus and started poking about, whilst others disappeared under the bonnet, or lay on the ground to inspect the undercarriage. Honestly, Lewis Hamilton's pit crew couldn't have been faster or more thorough.

There was a lot of shouting and professional-sounding comparing of notes and after a couple of minutes a yell and one of the boys emerged holding his nose in one hand and a large dead rat by the tail in the other.

"Is dead in engine," Marlene explained. "Is going in for warm, is dead, and is smell. Now is gone. No more problem, Sister. All OK."

And, after a couple of miles to blow the air through, it really was OK. So now, although the minibus is crumbling and doesn't like to start in the mornings, at least it doesn't smell of dead rat. It is a small mercy, but we are truly grateful for it.

To show our gratitude to the Lithuanians I gave them English tokens. These are an invention of Sister Bernard's. They are printed tickets saying, "We promise to give the holder on demand free English lessons". All they have to do is come to the Shoppe and I will dig out my Entry Level Activities workbook and off we will go! A remarkable number of them are fully-qualified engineers, so they learn fast.

I will start with, "Help! There is a rat in my van!" It works well phonically and it uses (as they put it on my training course) "the context of the learner's everyday life" – and the teacher's too, in this case.

I am enclosing with this letter four pairs of net curtains donated by the homeless recyclers – they should be just what you need for the mosquito netting. Let us know when we can help with anything else, and blessings to you all.

Best wishes,
Sister B.

29

LOBSTERS

Dear Sister Emelda,

I write at the end of a day full of surprises. As soon as the Shoppe opened at 8am, in strode Bob Fairbrother from the business units next door. He said, "Sister, I have a problem."

Now, Gertrude and I were on the Counselling in the Community workshop together at Walsingham last Spring, so I instantly recognised this as a "counselling moment" and said, in my counsellor voice, "Would you like to talk about it, Bob?"

"I would!" he replied. "My problem is lobsters."

I must admit that this turned a counselling moment into a Salvador Dali moment for me. "Lobsters?" I said.

"Six of them," said Bob. "Well only five are a problem, I'll eat one myself. How are you for fridge space? I'd like to give you five lobsters. They're worth about sixty pounds each. They were a present from a grateful Japanese client. I took the liberty of laminating you a little sign."

He whipped out a smart little sign, which said, "Top Quality Japanese Lobster, Fresh Today, £65 each".

I said, "That is extremely generous of you Mr Fairbrother, but not many of our customers ask for lobster. I'm not sure I'll be able to sell them in time."

"You'll sell them, Sister, don't you worry," he said. "I'll send them over in ten."

Now Emelda, perhaps you know more of these things than I, but I had no idea how large lobsters were. These animals were giants with enormously long feelers waving about in the box – because of course they were alive. They had elastic bands around their vast claws, but they waved them in protest all the same. I put them into the cold store and they and their boxes took up every inch.

I must admit the creatures filled me with sorrow. There was something terrible about their being on the Japanese sea bed peacefully waving their feelers about one day, and in my cold store with elastic bands on their claws the next. Rev Mother could only agree when she came by.

"I'll offer it up at Compline," she said. "Don't worry, Sister, there must be a purpose at work, and we'll find it."

You know what she's like, Emelda, the IMF would be far better off – and lots more cheerful – if she ever decided to drop the religious life and run the World Bank.

At about 8.30 a young woman I vaguely recognised came into the Shoppe with a camera and said,

"I'm Tilly Matthews. I work for *Beautiful Homes and Interiors* magazine, and we're doing an East Anglia feature next month and we wondered if we could take a few shots of the convent. Obviously we'd make a donation."

I said she was welcome, but what exactly did she want to "shoot" and when?

"Can I have a wander?" she asked.

I was about to say, no, wandering about wasn't really…when I saw Sister Gertrude on her way to the green bins and Tilly leapt with excitement and said, "Oh! May I?" and started photographing Sister Gertrude trundling her wheelbarrow.

Actually the composition was rather lovely. There was Gertrude in her long habit and wellies with a nicely rusted old barrow piled with vegetable peelings, slowly ambling down the avenue of beeches with the autumn light softly filtering through the russet leaves and highlighting her old red gardening gloves… But wait! Sister G might not take kindly to her image being purloined and put into…

"I must have a word!" cried Tilly and ran after Gertrude waving her camera. I feared the very worst. Nobody wants to be "papped" on their way to the compost – Gertrude's well into her seventies and she's not had Judy Dench's training.

Before I could do anything I was hailed by Green Rod in his wellies, buying shortbread to sustain his student workforce. They're checking the reed bed filtration system. He said, "I had no idea you stocked lobsters." I explained about Mr Fairbrother. GR peered into one of the boxes and said, "It's probably about thirty years old, a lovely specimen. My partner works at the SeaWorld Centre, she did her PhD on these chaps. Seems a shame. But can't look a gift horse in the mouth, I suppose."

So the lobsters turn out to be older than Hermione Baxter, our novice, who overheard and had tears running down her face by the time I had helped her unload today's kohlrabi. By the way, Emelda, do you have any advice about kohlrabi? We have a bumper harvest, and they're lovely-looking things, but Sister Gertrude boiled one for an hour yesterday and it was still quite hard. We usually make anything intransigent into tasty soup, as many of our visitors will remember, but these kohlrabi seem to resist even that. Shall we grate them raw? I have a lovely decorative pile of them in the Shoppe, but they're not going quickly, and it's partly because when people ask what to do with them I have to say I haven't really got any idea. (Bob Fairbrother would no doubt tell me that was very poor marketing, but it happens to be true.)

Anyway, by mid-morning I was beginning to imagine I could hear the mournful clacking of lobsters from inside their polystyrene prisons and Hermione had had to go and lie down, so things were not looking good. To make matters worse still Tilly had disappeared into the grounds with her camera and I was expecting if not complaints, exactly, then perhaps reproaches from startled sisters who didn't want to end up in *Beautiful Homes and Interiors*, even in long shot.

And every ten minutes all morning someone had come into the Shoppe, seen the sign, and felt they had to tell me how lobsters scream when they're boiled. Depending on their temperament, the person offering me this fact either suggested it was agonising pain that caused this, or that boiling was actually perfectly painless for the lobsters and the scream was caused by air escaping from their shell. If that's true, I'm a Dutchman, as my grand-dad used to say.

For a while around noon there were no customers in sight, so I wandered over to the reed beds where Rod and his team were taking samples. They were very cheerful as their theories, apparently, were all being proved accurate, and the convent water was as pure as pure after all the plants had filtered it. "Lovely when something so simple actually works," Rod sighed. "Any luck with the lobsters?"

I said no, and that we were asking for heavenly advice. Then I saw a car pull in to the Shoppe and left them counting water fleas.

The customer was lovely Amanda Forbes, who runs the gastro pub in the village. She said, "Kohlrabi, what luck! Nothing like it in a slaw. Can you let me have five? And I need carrots and some of your delightful white cabbage – let's say two kilos of each. Oh, and a sack of those lovely pink spuds of yours. We've got a rush on – huge delegation from Korea, something to do with the Science Park. Good business, but a bit of a hassle. Oh, lobster! What a thought that is. I could, mmm..." And she began inventing lobster menus and apparently doing little calculations on her mobile phone. I packed her vegetables into her big trolley and when I went to the till she said, "Oh go on then, I'll take three."

Emelda, that's £195! I did have a heavy heart, but I loaded the lobsters into Amanda's car and waved her off with them.

At about two, Sister Clementine came in to deliver a gateau and choose some vegetables for supper. "We have visitors tonight, Sister – Fathers Benjamin and Rudolfo from the Benedictines." She laughed. "Perhaps I should offer them a little lobster! But no, they are too simple for such luxury, I think! Ah, when I was younger, how often I cooked them in my aunt's kitchen at Valloris. Ah, what food! But these thoughts must not distract me. I must return with the lovely kohlrabi and leeks, and thank God for them on the way. See you later!"

I peeped in at the last two lobsters and prayed for an easy resolution. When Rod passed I asked him if lobsters could swim very far. He said, "No, they sort of walk along the ocean bed, I think, mostly. Sometimes there are mysterious armies of them spotted marching along in formation. Nobody has ever worked out how they communicate, but they certainly do. They're very ancient and interesting. They have been recorded as living to ninety years old. Some researchers believe that they could actually live indefinitely..."

"I've just sold three to the Rising Lark," I blurted out.

"Well, they definitely won't live to be ninety, then. But it's a boost to the local economy and somebody will certainly enjoy them, I suppose. Did I mention my wife worked at the Sea World Centre? She might be able to…"

"Lobsters! Oh, bliss!" This was Tilly Matthews bustling back in her pretty wellingtons. "I'll have one, Sister. It's just what I fancy after a hard day."

"They're live," I said, in case it put her off.

"Oh, don't worry about that. I always poke a knitting needle into their brain first. A little trick a chef once taught me."

She's all frills and flowery lace; you'd never guess to look at her.

At least the poor thing wouldn't suffer for long. I loaded it into Tilly's car with a brief blessing.

"Thanks so much, sisters," called Tilly. "I have some lovely shots and I'll be sure to send a complimentary copy of next month's mag. Oh, and here's a little donation. Enjoy!" She handed me an envelope, which I dropped into the till.

So that left just one lobster in the cold store. Rev Mother and I were looking at it sadly when Rod came in to tell us he was off to report a state of rude health in the reed beds. "Flora and fauna all thriving, sisters. Congratulations."

"What a shame a lobster couldn't live there," said Rev Mother.

Rod said, "No, they need the sea. It could live at the Sea World Centre, though. There's room in the tank – I checked with Rosie."

So lobster number five, at least, lives on. He is settled in the Sea World Centre, where he is among his own kind and Doctor Rosie can examine him periodically (but not in an invasive way, I'm assured) and add to the world's surprisingly limited knowledge of lobsters.

When she cashed up, Nesbitt spotted and opened Tilly's little envelope. It contained £300.

£560 in a single day. We can send for underwear and pay at least a down payment on the dentist's bill. There's even enough to add something to the Bell Tower fund. Result! (as Nesbitt would say.)

Best wishes,
Sister B.

30

ARRESTED

Dear Wanderer,

Our favourite hen, Joan of Ark, has just hatched five chicks very late in the season. They are all different and follow her everywhere, peeping so loudly that we could even hear them in chapel yesterday between prayers of thanks for the newly mended roof. We have moved all the buckets out of the dining room and can eat together around the great table for the first time in months.

Pavel was invited inside to see how his handiwork has changed our mealtimes, and he came shyly in and bowed solemnly to everyone he met. It will be a quieter place without him. Nesbitt has enjoyed making him huge picnics three times a day, and she's been very inventive with the sandwich fillings. Carmella will certainly miss him. She enjoyed their chats.

He refused any money. All we could persuade him to accept was a little box of supplies and a chocolate cake made by Sister Clementine. She volunteered, casually saying at convocation, "Oh, that is no problem. I have made one or two before. It will be nothing. So hard he has worked. It will be my pleasure."

Well! She brought it round to the Shoppe that afternoon and I was astonished! It was perfection! Glossily iced, immaculately presented, sitting on a little silver base (wherever did she find that?) with a delicate lilac ribbon around it.

"I hope he will not mind a sachertorte," she said. "It is long since I made one, but one does not forget. The trick is to make the…what is this word?"

"Icing?" I suggested.

"Yes, the icing very smooth, crisp and shiny. I was successful, I believe."

"But how did you learn?" I asked.

She laughed. "Oh! My father is a pastry chef, a patissier. I grew up in the shop. But I left all that behind long ago. Still, now and then, it is permitted."

She was so modest that she retired before the cake was presented, so she did not see Pavel take the beautiful cake in his giant hands and gaze at it in wonder. He offered in mime to cut it there and then and share it with us all, but we insisted he should carry it away whole. We waved him off and watched him trudge off down the lane with his rucksack full of tools, carrying the cake the way the three kings bear their gifts in that famous Titian painting.

"Wonder where he lives?" Nesbitt said, as we cashed up.

I had to admit I'd never really thought.

"Only I sometimes see him in the morning coming through that gap in Odge's hedge by the old pear tree."

"Maybe he's got some work with Odge," I suggested. "I hope so."

She wrote the float into the cashbook.

"Maybe he's going to do some picking for him. He always gets his strawberry pickers from foreign places, doesn't he?"

"Does he?" I said. "Wouldn't local people be glad of that work?"

"You ever tried strawberry picking?" she asked. "It's awful work, you have to bend double all day and even if you're good at it, the money's rubbish. My mum used to do it years ago, and she picked potatoes too, but nobody from round here wants to do it now."

So in our minds Pavel was going cheerfully off to another job, even if it was not a very well paid one, which as it turns out, was wrong.

Two days later we were listing our order for Hedgeby when we heard a great wailing of police sirens. Nothing drove past our turning, so the trouble, whatever it was, must be up the lane at Odge's Farm.

Hermione said, "You don't think it could be Hilda on her bike, do you? Or rather off her bike." Which filled us with anxiety because Hilda rides her moped to and from town every day and we do worry about her in the traffic. So we sent Hermione off up the lane to make sure it wasn't, and she ran back in two minutes and said, "Oh, Sister, I think they're arresting Pavel."

I rushed up the lane in time to see our poor handcuffed builder being piled into the back of a police car. There must have been half a dozen police vehicles and at least twenty officers. Rev Mother followed us up the lane, which I was glad of; she's the sort of commanding figure even police officers automatically respond to. Her size helps, but it's more a case of natural authority.

"And you are...?" demanded a senior-looking police officer.

"I am Elizabeth, Reverend Mother of St Winifreda's," declared our leader in her best don't-mess-with-us-nuns sort of way. "You appear to be arresting a man of very good character."

"Inspector Ronald Swift," countered the officer, with the momentary hesitation lots of people show as they decide whether or not to shake hands with religious sisters. Rev Mother solved this by grasping his firmly.

"You know him?" asked Swift.

"Yes. He's just finished repairing our roof. And a fine job he did of it too."

"You employed him?"

"On a voluntary basis."

"You didn't pay him then?

"No. We gave him food. What is the trouble?"

"Mr Odge's foreman found him living rough in his old chicken shed. Thought he was on the run or something. Illegal, anyway."

Rev Mother looked shocked. "Was Odge housing him in a chicken shed?"

"Didn't know anything about him," said Swift. "Nobody did. Looks as if he's been there for a few weeks."

She looked even more shocked. "So all the time he was working on our roof, he was living rough?"

"Yes. We get a lot of it, actually. They come over here, can't find a job, have to sleep rough. There're whole camps of them hidden away. Surprisingly neat, most of them, too."

Swift was relaxing a little, but then caught himself and went on, "Can't be allowed, obviously."

"What will happen to him?"

"We'll run some checks to make sure he's not wanted for any crime, then probably just send him home – back to his country. Unless there are any charges pressed."

"What sort of charges?"

"Mr Odge might want him charged with criminal damage, if he's done any harm to the chicken shed."

At this point Odge drove up in one of his huge vehicles and jumped out. From the end of the lane all we saw was Rev Mother speak briefly to him before the three figures, one black, one blue and one tweedy green, moved aside in deep conversation.

Hermione and Nesbitt brought sandwiches and coffee up in the wheelbarrow and handed them round. Uniformed officers always appreciate sustenance. They said things like, "Don't mind if I do",

"Wouldn't say no", and "Very generous, we'll have to come more often!"

But our dear friend was still arrested, and the jolly atmosphere did not extend to him. He sat pale and silent in the police van.

I came back to take care of the Shoppe and I write this in some distress, imagining how heedless we have been to the hardships of our good-hearted volunteer. I fear we have exploited him, Emelda. We were so grateful for the roof being repaired at last that we didn't give a thought to the wellbeing of our worker. God forgive us all.

Please pray that we can find some way of making amends.

Best wishes,
Sister B.

31

THE POLICE STATION

Dear Happy Holy Wandering Spirit,

Your parcel from Santo Domingo was very welcome. It arrived just as we were struggling with shame over our treatment of our volunteer. The children's drawings you sent are now decorating the Shoppe and I have sold three of the tiny boxes already. They are exquisite and have a beautiful scent, but we can't quite work out what they are made of. Nesbitt thinks it may be orange peel – is she right?

Father Humbert sends his regards. He is up and about now that the walking plaster is on.

After Pavel was driven away, we were so ashamed of our mistreatment of him that we had an emergency convocation and decided the only way we could immediately show solidarity was to go to the police station and take some food and warm clothing. It wasn't much, but it was all we could think of.

So while Rev Mother continued her discussions with Odge, four of us drove to town in the minibus and went to the police station with our care parcels.

We would give him the gifts and pray with him to cheer him up, we thought.

The police officers on reception were a bit taken aback by our arrival. They said visitors were not allowed. We said Pavel was an innocent man and had done nothing to anyone, so why should visitors not be allowed?

They tried to fill out forms.

"Title?"

"Sister."

"Name?"

"Boniface"

"Surname?"

"I don't use one."

"Sarge, how do I fill this in?"

The sergeant sighed and said, "Leave it to me, McIntosh."

"Purpose of visit?"

"To comfort a prisoner."

"Name of prisoner?"

"Pavel."

"Surname?"

"Um. Sorry, we don't know for sure, it begins with 'Sz'... It's hard to say and much harder to spell."

"So you nuns who don't have surnames want to visit a prisoner who also doesn't have a surname?"

"Yes, please."

"How's that going to look in the paperwork?"

"Can't we just give him the parcel? It has sandwiches and cake and a jumper in it. We can show you if you like."

"It's security, you see. We can't let you in without searching you."

"We don't mind being searched."

"I'll just call the Inspector."

And so it went on. We had extra sandwiches and cake, so we gave them to the other people in the waiting area, which had a sign saying, "Designated Waiting Area – Do Not Cross Yellow Line Until Called".

It was quite late now on a Saturday evening and most of the other people waiting were in distress, so they were glad of the sandwiches, and a boy with a big tattoo told another one to mind his language. It was a disinfectant-smelling place and the seats were hard and everything was nailed down, which Eustacia said was for health and safety so that nothing could be thrown or broken over anyone's head; she used work at Pentonville.

But we decided just to stay until they either let us see Pavel or actually forced us to leave, so we just said a few rosaries and the time actually passed quite cheerfully. In fact because there were four of us, we took over the waiting area, really, and Eustacia can't help organising people, so she started welcoming newcomers in and introducing everybody.

"Come in, Liz. This is Steve and this is Timo and Vinnie. If you just sit there – that's it, hold on tight. They'll be with you in a jiffy, won't you, Constable McIntosh?"

I suppose we were there about three hours. Then without any sort of warning the door opened and the Sergeant led Pavel in.

"There are no charges. He can go," he said. "But he can't sleep rough. Do I need to find a hostel?"

We said no, we'd find somewhere. We weren't sure where, but we said goodbye to all our police station friends, packed back into the minibus and drove back to St Winifreda's. And when we arrived, tired and in the case of the builder, shocked and disoriented, we were met by Rev Mother who told us Odge would let him stay, at least for a few days, in an old field workers' caravan.

So our friend is free, at least for now.

In convocation the next day we decided that although we could certainly offer him work, we could not possibly allow him to do it for food for any longer. He needs to be paid money. We are not sure where it will come from, but it will have to be found.

Your prayers are welcome, as ever,

Best wishes,
Sister B.

32

THE PIGPENS

Dear Wanderer,

Last Tuesday Pavel came into the Shoppe and said, "Sister, is little house there near wall?" He pointed over towards the northeast wall where the old pigpens once were.

I said, "Little house? No, I don't think so."

"But I see little house," he insisted. "I see" – he mimed an upright pipe shape – "from roof I see that."

"Oh, a chimney. No, it's not a house, it's the old pig pens."

"Is nobody live in?"

"No," I explained. "It was where they kept the pigs. Just outside the wall. They're derelict now. Empty. Overgrown, broken, lots of trees, brambles, empty for years and years."

"Pigs?" Pavel was puzzled.

Nesbitt made a very convincing pig snort in the background.

"Ah! Pigs!" He thought for a while.

"I fix? Live in? Fix. Yes?"

"But they're houses for pigs," I said.

"Before I live in chickens' house. Maybe pigs' house is better!"

There was logic in this. I told him I'd have to see what the other sisters said.

So at convocation I asked about the pigpens, and Eustacia said, "Why on earth would pigpens have chimneys?"

"Um, actually, I can answer that," Hermione said. "They were actually houses. They appear as cottages up until the..." she leafed through a file she had on her lap "...the 1943 map, the convent used them to house Land Girls during the War. But by 1955 they are shown as pigpens, so I suppose nobody wanted to live in them and they used them for pigs instead."

"Perhaps we could get permission to restore them," Rev Mother said. "Odge is on the Parish Council, he'll know."

He checked and found out that since the pigpens were once houses, planning permission shouldn't be a problem. On Friday the community service workers (bristling with protective gear) began chopping through a half century of brambles and found the three tumbledown cottages. One had been used for pigs, but the other two were just shut up, overgrown and damp.

"Just right for bed and breakfast rooms!" remarked Rev Mother. "Shall we call them the Pigpens or re-name them?"

Talk about vision, Emelda! The rest of us saw dereliction and mildew; she saw lovely guest accommodation.

We will have to supply materials for the restoration work, but so far Pavel has found most things he needs lying about unused in our outhouses. Green Rod has become involved and every time he arrives with his students they unload all sorts of recycled bits and pieces from the van. I definitely saw a length of guttering and a sink go in yesterday. People throw amazing things away. The community service workers will do the painting and the clearing is already coming on very well. We know the progress because we deliver sandwiches and cups to tea to them all.

Animal and Baz have set to with zeal. "We love clearance, don't we, Baz? You know where you are with clearance. No fiddly bits to get you into trouble."

"Get *you* into trouble," yelled Baz from behind an enormous thicket. "You break anything smaller than a billhook."

Alphonsus is rarely with them because he is now officially working on the convent computer system, donated by Roger Collis at Intermediax – who seems to think nothing of parting with perfectly good computers no more than three years old.

"Can't have you using those old dinosaurs," Collis told Sr Bernard. "You need something more reliable if you're going online. Time your computers came into the twenty-first century!"

The big surprise for me has been people's enthusiasm for the sandwiches we now sell in the Shoppe.

Our customers love a sandwich – especially if hand-crafted by the ever-inventive Nesbitt. She's in early every morning and humming away in the back room turning out piles of egg mayonnaise with chorizo, rocket and tomato with mozzarella, olive paste with tuna and sundried tomato. Forget the fish paste or jam type of thing we used to eat on beach picnics in my youth; Nesbitt is a maker of posh sandwiches.

And it turns out the villagers of Three Fens, along with the office workers and the pickers from Odge's Farm have all been craving a posh sandwich for ages; we can hardly sell them fast enough. Hari was impressed. He came last week for my post-course assessment and ticked every box on his checklist with a happy smile.

"Value adding! Sister! That is the way! You take basic ingredients, bread, eggs…"

"…focaccia, mortadella, bresaola," chimed in Nesbitt.

"Well, perhaps not quite so basic…and then you add value through your labour. This is a fine example of supplying market demand through sheer creative ingenuity."

"The ingenuity is all Nesbitt's," I said. "I think it should be Nesbitt who gets all the marks for this."

Nesbitt laughed and returned to the back room to create more value-adding sandwiches.

"There is a point in what you say," Hari replied, confidentially. "Is Miss Nesbitt taking any qualification? It would be good practice if you ensured that your employee gained an NVQ. I am aware that she is a volunteer, but that should be no bar to her education. I always ensure that all my employees are given encouragement in this area."

I said I would look into it and then had to serve Amanda Forbes who was buying up mange tout for the Rising Lark – another tick from Hari for joining the local supply chain and selling peas to the gastro pub.

"Ah, Sister, I see you are like a duck in water now. What a wonderful thing it is to use our talents for the greater good."

"You have a very noble-minded way of looking at the world, Hari," I told him. "I have no natural gift for this at all."

"Why, Sister Boniface, releasing the gifts in those around us is a particularly special talent. In my faith there is a saying: He who frees a dove takes flight himself."

It is a sentiment I like very much – without fully understanding. Perhaps it makes sense to you, Emelda. Anyway, top marks for the Shoppe, and all because of Nesbitt. I raised the matter of her education in the convocation that evening, pointing out that she was working many hours a week for no pay.

"Good Lord, Boniface, don't we pay her, either?" Rev Mother asked. "We seem to make a habit of accepting people's unpaid labour."

I said, "She likes the work, she just helps out when she can."

"Shouldn't she be at school or something?" asked Sr Patrick.

"She's left school," I said. "There's very little work around here. She's unemployed, technically."

"And how many hours does she give us at the Shoppe?"

"Well," I said, "that's just it. At first it was just a couple of hours now and then, but since we started selling the cake and sandwiches she's had to work longer and longer to keep up with demand."

"Oh dear, are we guilty of exploiting someone else? I do hope not," said Rev Mother.

"Is she content? Does she enjoy this work?" Sister Clementine asked.

"She seems to enjoy it very much," I told her. "She comes in with lists of new sandwich ideas and she loves to talk to Carmella about what there is in the garden. She takes a real pleasure in it all."

"Well, that is something. At least we are not slave-drivers," Rev Mother said. "We'll pray on this one for a couple of days, but I think we should ask for a decision by the end of the week."

Our other undertaking has been to offer Pavel some English lessons. It's easy enough – three of us at the convent have teaching qualifications – and it's something he can really benefit from. We've already started. Every evening at 6 we open up the mini classroom behind the Shoppe and in he troops, often with a couple of friends from Odge's Farm, for a lesson. So far we have focused on the vocabulary of food and polite requests like, "Cake, please"!

Annunziata says the dish you asked about is called yaguarlocro; it is potato soup with blood. Quite nice if you've been brought up with it, apparently. (I'm enclosing some cup-a-soups as an alternative.)

Best wishes,
Sister B.

33

KABUKI

Dear Sister Emelda,

Your last letter reached us in an appalling state: stained, torn, scrawled with re-directions and covered in indecipherable stamps. We feared a raid by brigands at the South American end, but the postman said it was the new sorting machine in March playing up. Either that or Wilf reversed the van over the sack again. He's a good old boy, but according to Mr Dunn he doesn't know what his mirrors are for.

Thought of brigands did make us worry about your safety, Emelda. I know long experience of bringing prayer to disaster areas and lawless backwaters stands you in good stead, but would you like a bullet-proof vest to wear? We found a pattern on the internet and Mother Matilda is pretty sure she can run one up from materials to hand. You can wear them under or over. Just say the word and we'll pop one in the post – it should be tough enough to survive even Wilf and his post van.

I have just lined up a special treat for Pavel who is climbing all over the convent buildings today blocking rat holes. It is a plate of Sister Clementine's latest biscuits. The list keeps on growing. When we discussed the idea of baking our own special St Winifreda's biscuit everyone had a different idea of what it should be.

So far we've had lemony ones and treacly ones and shortbread and a chunky thing based on a Dorset Knob, which I didn't like the look of at all. We've had Llamas and St W?innies and Guinea Pigs with raisins. Today we have just the kind of slim, elegant little delicacy you might expect from a French patissier's daughter. They smell of orange. I can't wait to see Pavel's face – although I suspect he will consider twenty of them only a pre-snack.

Really, the rats have begun to depress our spirits terribly by nibbling and gnawing all night long as well as scampering about the corridors in the most shameless and proprietorial way. On Monday in chapel I watched one canter down the aisle and pause insouciantly two inches from Mother Hilda's hassock to clean its whiskers. Mercifully my dear sisters were all praying too devoutly to notice.

We have decided to wage war on them by blocking their entry points. It takes a real expert to spot these – they can be tiny – and the convent is a big place and one with plenty of holes at all levels, so they've had a happy time until now. The thing is, Emelda, we can't use poison because we read about it on the internet and whilst effective it is also appalling. It does things I can't even mention to their insides and they die in agony and if they do so out of doors owls eat them and then they die too, so we can't bear it.

A rat here and there is no problem to us, so we have decided just to try to keep their numbers down and keep them well out of the Shoppe and the kitchen. We are all praying that they see the sense in this and co-operate. Your prayers would be welcome too!

Yesterday we were blessed with something very surprising – a Japanese coach party! Their coach limped into the yard and the driver, a local man, explained that he was having trouble with his exhaust and needed to stop somewhere and send for a mechanic. Could the Japanese visitors come into the Shoppe and perhaps sit in the garden while he waited? Of course they could, poor things.

They piled out and turned out to be – can you imagine this, Emelda? – a touring Kabuki theatre group.

I was up to my elbows in sandwiches when Sister Gertrude, who had been taking their orders, reported this to me. She was full of excitement. It is a very noble and mysterious art form apparently, and very spiritually uplifting. In Sadlers Wells (she worked there in her youth) they put Kabuki plays on every year and aficionados come from all over. I was a bit busy hoping they would like ham because we were short of cheese, so some of the detail was lost on me, but it all sounded very interesting.

The visitors sat in the garden – it was a sunny day, luckily, and we took them trays of tea and sandwiches.

They were shy at first, not perhaps being used to convents or religious sisters, but then they cheered up and began to sing. At first they sang together in a folk song sort of way, but gradually they seemed to start taking roles and soon it was what seemed to be a play.

The leading actor was a quite elderly man, treated with utmost respect by everyone in the party. He assumed a strange position and sang in a terrible and strange high-pitched voice, moving his hands and head and rolling his eyes. It was thrilling and dreadful at the same time. They had no musicians because they were on the other bus and halfway to Norwich, so all the actors sang the music, including imitating drums and cymbals.

Other customers who had dropped into the Shoppe for some milk or a few potatoes were hypnotised by the performance; the strange music seemed to hang in the air around the convent for a long time after their bus was mended and they left.

Meanwhile they had spent a small fortune in the Shoppe on refreshments and especially on souvenirs. They favoured Sister Emily's decorated clothes pegs – about forty of them went – and also Mother Mary Divine's lovely embroidered bookmarks.

What a day. I must hurry now to get the retired sisters' TV turned on in time, and to make sure we avoid *Crimewatch*, or worse still, their latest nightmare – *The X Factor*!

Best wishes,
Sister B.

34

Mother Hilda's Lessons

Dear Wanderer,

We loved your description of the dawn chorus in the jungle, with the horned screamer birds that sound like drowning donkeys and the frogs with calls like electronic beepers. Here we say our morning prayers to John Paul the cockerel's crowing and the soft hum of trucks on the A10. There are frogs too, now that the reed beds are working.

It is still warm enough to work in the garden. Yesterday I helped Carmella pick a few flowers for the first guests in the Pigpens.

They are quite finished now and the rooms are lovely. Hard to believe the convent's pigs had them to themselves for half a century. No trace of a smell (in case you were wondering). We had a big debate about the furnishings. None of us has much experience in soft furnishings, but the consensus was that cushions were very important and there had to be a certain amount of matching in the fabrics.

I tried to recall what *Ideal Homes* said about bedrooms, but couldn't remember much except that "rustic" and "shaker" were both favoured as styles – which ought to have been easy for us to achieve – but turned out to be really expensive. I was puzzling over this when Tilly Matthews in her flowery wellies dropped in to the Shoppe with our free copies of *Beautiful Homes and Interiors* magazine.

"Hi, Sister B," she said. "I hope you don't mind, I put the website address on. It's the usual thing and it might bring you some customers. It, like, really helps some people with their business and everything."

"How are you on soft furnishings, Tilly?" I asked.

"Oh, in my element!" she cried. "Absolutely my thing. Ask away."

In ten minutes she had listed everything we needed from throws (whatever they are) to rugs, vases and shaker coat hooks.

"It couldn't be easier, Sister. Look, all the suppliers are here in the back of the mag!"

"We have a budget of fifty pounds." I said.

"Fifty pounds? What, for everything?"

"Well, not the furniture itself, that's coming from the homeless recyclers in Water Lode, but the soft furnishings, yes. Fifty pounds in total."

"OMG," said Tilly. "Fifty pounds! Now that is a challenge. Can I 'before and after' it?"

"Can you what?"

"Take 'before' and 'after' pics for the mag?"

"Yes, I suppose so."

"OK, now we're talking. Are you happy to leave the choices to me? I'll have to use whatever I can get. Might be a bit…eclectic."

"Eclectic is fine, I said, as long as it's within the budget."

I gave her a sample box of Guinea Pigs and off she went, buzzing with excitement.

Three days later a van pulled up and Tilly and her team unloaded a small mountain of objects into the new rooms. An afternoon was spent arranging and photographing them, and when I visited, the effect was quite dazzling.

"Well, Tilly said," with a sigh of satisfaction, "we all have our thing, Sister. This is mine. I called in a few favours and there was an amazing amount of stuff just lying around the office. People send us things."

I handed over the £50 with our grateful thanks.

"Oh, nothing to it," she said. "I had fun. I'll put the website on the piece again. Good luck with the bookings! And by the way, those biscuits were delish! Put them on the website, I'd buy them any time."

So, all there was left to do was to hang the "Bed and Breakfast" sign underneath the Convent Shoppe sign in the lane. I did this at 6pm after closing and at 6.16 Rute and Angele Van Holdt rolled up. Our first guests.

"Were they sitting in the lane praying for a bed for the night, do you think?" Hermione wondered. "How could they know?"

But they did, and most nights now someone finds us. Hermione does a lot of the B&B work, but Sister Lakmini from Sri Lanka has offered to cook breakfasts. So, St Winifreda's is officially in the bed and breakfast business. And that's another box ticked on the self-sufficiency checklist, as Rev Mother remarked!

It is Mother Hilda's saint's day today and we believe it is her hundredth. We're not absolutely sure and she has little interest, being too busy visiting the elderly most of the time. It was only six months ago that she gave up making her rounds by bicycle and accepted the offer of Father O'Reardon's old moped.

We clubbed together to buy her a helmet and a few motorcycling lessons from a nice man in the village, Big Lee, who rides a very throaty motorbike and sometimes stops into the Shoppe. He has a lot of tattoos, but he was kindness itself to Hilda and they spent several afternoons riding slowly up and down the gardens before he led her out onto the road.

When he decided she was safe to venture out alone he insisted on giving her a full set of his old leathers. Mother Matilda and her seamstresses rose wonderfully to the challenge of cutting them down to fit Hilda, who is approximately one sixth of Big Lee's size, so now she is fully outfitted and zooms off every day laden with gifts and good wishes and everyone in the village loves to see her.

Lee had a skull and crossbones on the back of the jacket, but we painted them out and put a big white cross on instead, partly as a high-viz safety feature and partly to identify Hilda to passing motorists in the hope that they might give her the benefit of the doubt. We added the number "100" in luminous paint to it yesterday.

Anyway, Sister Clementine is making a cherry cake, Hilda's favourite, and I am trying to complete a cross-stitch glasses case, but I am still as weak a needlewoman as ever. I do try. I pray for patience, but the Lord must intend me for other things – otherwise why would He make the undersides of everything I sew such a tangle? Knotty undersides: metaphor for life or just poor needlecraft? Discuss!

Blessings and good wishes,
Sister B.

Convent Shoppe Assistant and (since last week) Pig Pen Accommodation Bookings Clerk

35

THE POORE PASTURE

Dear Emelda,

A beautiful autumn here. The vine that grows over the porch has turned exactly the red of Delilah's dress in the Rubens. Delilah Red. I saw it four decades ago, but you never forget. Here in the Shoppe I am surrounded by Sister Carmella's next impressive crop of pumpkins. Some are grey/blue and taste of chestnut; some are seamed or striped; others are shaped like a curled trumpet. Nesbitt is very skillful at making harvest festival-style displays. I have just taken a photograph of one for Father Humbert, who is laid up with a sprained ankle. He misjudged the steps at school assembly and needs cheering up.

As I look closely I notice a number of pipe-cleaner priests peeping out. I sold seven priests and eight pumpkins yesterday. Hard to say whether the tiny priests help to sell the pumpkins, or the other way round.

Hermione arrived breathless in the Shoppe just now. "Have I missed Rev Mother?" she asked.

"She's measuring ground source cable runs with Green Rod, I think," I told her.

"I want to show her this. It's the only set of actual deeds I've managed to find. Somebody called Robert Woodgate gave us a piece of land. Look!" She showed me a document in curly handwriting and a little hand-drawn map showing a triangular piece of land. The artist had helpfully drawn a couple of cows grazing on it. Then Baz came in for elevenses, so I had to get on.

At convocation Hermione showed everyone the document and read it out.

"*In the name of God, Amen, I Robert Woodgate of Hogge Fenn, In the County of Suffolk, Considering the uncertainety of life being desierous to setel my wordly affairs and leave peace behind me after my decease, do make and ordaine this my last will and testament...*"

"Is this going to take long?" asked Eustacia. "Only Sister Mary Loyola's in sick bay with a temperature."

"Go on, Hermione," said Rev Mother.

"*...my last will and testament in maner and form following: that is to say ffirst I Commend my Soule into the hand of my Creator hopeing through his mercy to have a Joyfull resurrection to Life Eternal, and my body I Commit to the earth to be decently buried at the Discretion of my Executor hearin afternamed, and such worldly estate as God has bestowed on mee I Give and dispose as ffolloweth;*"

We all leaned in closer.

Hermione continued, "*I Give and bequeath and devize my pasture Ground Lieing within the ffields and bounds of King's Hedges north of Cambridge called the Poore Pasture Containing by Estimation five acre to the use and behoof of the sisterhood of St Winifredde at Hogge Fenn in perpetuity.*

To the library at the house of St Winifredde at Hogge Fenn I likewise bequeath My inlaiyd oaken chest with brass hinges and my books. It is my deseir that the oaken chest remain unopened until ffifty yeares have passed after the time of my death.

I give and bequeath unto my servants James Williams and Elisa Williams, his wife, the Sum of Twenty Pounds jointly to be paid unto them by my Executor. All the rest of my Goods and Chattles, and personal Estate whatsoever, I give and bequeath unto my brother Alexander Woodgate of Battisham, Suffolk whom I do hereby constitute and ordain the Executor of this my last Will and Testament: In Witness whereof I have hereunto set my Hand and Seal, this first Day of October in the year of our Lord one Thousand eight Hundred and sixty-eight.

Rev Mother was very taken with the drawing of the little cows too. "Isn't it just our luck that it's called the Poore Pasture and not the Ricche Meadows!" she said. "Do we still own it? Any idea where it might be? I'll let the Diocese know, anyway."

To judge from the drawing, the land is just about big enough for a couple of cows and one corner seems to be a marsh, so we're not pinning too many hopes on it. But an asset's and asset, and as Agnes pointed out, everything's sent for a reason.

This letter, for example, is sent to entertain you in your tireless labours for the poor children of La Santa. I hope it does!

Best wishes,
Sister B.

36

THE BISHOP VISITS

Dear Wanderer,

I will be enclosing a cheque for £45.67 in this letter! It is for the sale of your boxes. It's extraordinary to think of those tiny objects crafted so carefully by your villagers being posted all the way around the world to St Winifreda's. Even more extraordinary when you think that they are made of orange peel. The ingenuity!

I was just dusting the "Handmade Gifts" shelf this morning, when Rev Mother ran into the Shoppe and said breathlessly, "I've had a call from the Bishop's office. He's on his way to Norwich from Cambridge and he wondered if he and the diocesan committee could drop in for a flying site visit! At about eleven!"

This gave us barely forty-five minutes to prepare. Nesbitt and I tidied the Shoppe hurriedly, laid out a particularly lovely array of sandwiches, rolls and ciabattas and half a dozen of Sister Clem's cakes. We still have homemade bunting up around the place, and though I say it myself, it's a picture.

Through the convent windows I could see sisters hurrying and scurrying about, straightening curtains and waving down cobwebs from corners, and at precisely 11.07 up swept three cars, all large and dark, but one larger and darker than the rest. Rev Mother stepped forward and out climbed Bishop Sheringham himself. It was an informal visit, which meant, we were told, that we should all go about our work in the normal way and the Bishop and his team would do the rounds with Rev Mother and just say a quick blessing for us all on the way out.

From the Shoppe window we could see a welcome being given and an invitation to look around St Winifreda's. Twelve other priests climbed out of their cars and were taken straight into the visitors' parlour, where coffee was waiting. They were all talking to one another and carrying briefcases. Two of them lit cigarettes and stood outside the porch to smoke them.

Meanwhile we saw the Bishop point briskly to the Shoppe. He wanted to see the Shoppe! Nesbitt and I stood behind the counter, trying to look casual and business-like and welcoming and (in my case) serious and perhaps a little Godly too. He threw the door open.

"Well, what have we here? This shop is new," he said.

"Yes," said Rev Mother, with a hint of pride. "We've expanded over the past year."

"And you sell…?"

"Well, as you see, besides our own vegetables, we offer household goods and we also have a very successful line in lunchtime food like sandwiches, cake and biscuits," Rev Mother explained.

"Who buys them?" queried the Bishop, peering around.

"We are lucky enough to have a small business development just up the lane, here. There are about fifteen businesses with all their employees. And there are also the field workers from the neighbouring farm…"

"Is it profitable?"

"I'll allow Boniface to talk you through the finances," said Rev Mother, rather smoothly. "May I introduce Sister Boniface, who runs the Shoppe? Boniface, this is Bishop Tom Sheringham."

And then it happened. I was supposed to come round the counter, take his hand and offer him the traditional salutation by kissing his ring, but my foot caught the corner. I grabbed something to steady myself and it turned out to be a cake stand and one of the Lemon Drizzles – a particularly moist one, as it turned out – flipped off the top, rotated spectacularly in mid-air and landed wet and sticky on the Bishop's left shoulder. A large chunk then broke off, rolled down his waistcoat and splatted onto his highly polished shoe.

There was a terrible, motionless silence, followed by a flurry as Nesbitt dived for a cloth while Rev Mother and I set about apologising and removing lemony sponge from soft suiting. But before this happened there was a tiny second of communication – a fractional eye contact between Rev Mother and myself in which we both knew that, unless we were very careful, we were going to laugh.

The Bishop, on the other hand, was not finding the situation amusing at all.

"Oh, now that really is a terrible mess," he said. "I've to wear this all day and it'll be sticky. For goodness sake, leave it," he told Nesbitt, who was attempting to sponge his shoes. "I'll have to change. It'll mean a detour." But then he came to himself a little and said, "Well, it can't be helped. It was an accident. If you just send Father Donaldson over, he can make the arrangements. I expect someone can drive back and bring me something to change into."

Rev Mother went for help, and the Bishop finished flapping his handkerchief and, gathering himself, looked around the Shoppe once more. "Is it a money-spinner, then, your shop?"

"Well, it makes a profit, but not a large one." I told him.

"And is it what you want, Sister?"

"Sorry?"

"Is this how you expected your vocation to be? Shop keeping? Selling things? Do you not feel it is a distraction from your calling? We must all remember not to be diverted from our true way. Of course, money is needed. Nobody denies it. But consider the lilies of the field, Boniface. Do not put profit," he looked about him, "do not put French beans and mortadella before your soul. And who is this?"

"This is Nesbitt. She helps in the Shoppe."

"Are you homeless?" he asked, benignly. "A young offender?"

"No I…" Poor Nesbitt couldn't get her words out.

"Ah, disadvantaged," said the Bishop. "Learning difficulties. I see. Good work, Sister. But remember what I said about your soul. Goodbye."

And he left, slamming the door so hard that the open/closed sign flew off and broke on the floor. We were left standing like statues in a fragrant slush of lemon drizzle.

There was a snuffle from somewhere, and when I looked it was Nesbitt. She fiercely wiped her eyes with the back of her hand.

"He said I had learning difficulties," she said, quietly.

And God forgive me, Emelda, but I couldn't do it. I just couldn't allow anyone to trample so heedlessly on the feelings of someone as generous and hard working as Nesbitt. I knew that if I didn't say something, something very firm and strong, it would be the disagreeable train lady all over again, but this time far worse.

So, and I ask everyone's forgiveness of this in advance, I grabbed Nesbitt by the arm and rushed her out, and we intercepted the Bishop as he was passing the smokers outside the porch.

I had no idea how to start, so I just blurted out, "Bishop Sheringham, you are wrong!"

He braked and swerved, the slug trail of lemon drizzle on his jacket catching the sunlight.

I blundered on. "Nesbitt here, my co-worker in the Shoppe, is absolutely not disadvantaged and she has no difficulties in learning at all. She has worked tirelessly for us, and it is just not fair for you to insult her and walk away. She deserves better. She deserves an apology. She deserves (I was getting carried away) your humble thanks."

The two smokers now moved forward. One of them said, "Now, Sister, I don't think you should…" And the other, "Now steady on…" or words to that effect. The Bishop waved them away.

"I'm sure this is just a tiny misunderstanding," he told me. "I never intended any…" here he looked over his little glasses at Nesbitt "…any kind of slight to this young lady. I'm sure you're doing everyone a great service in your little Shoppe, Sister. We'll leave it at that, shall we?"

And with that he spun and entered the front door, followed by a striding wall of suited priests.

Rev Mother was just inside. She had seen the whole thing. She swivelled to follow the visitors and I was left with an impression of her sweeping robes.

Nesbitt shifted and I realised I was still grasping her sleeve.

"Bloody 'ell, Sister!" she said. "That told him."

"Did it?" I said. I wasn't sure.

"You stood up for me – against that Bishop!"

At this point Animal and Baz ambled up the south path and headed for the Shoppe. "Come on," she said. "Customers!"

So we went back to work, cutting slabs of cake and selling sandwiches to the community service workers.

"Who's that geezer in the big motor?" asked Animal genially.

"That's the Bishop," said Nesbitt. "He was rude to me and Sister B gave him a telling off."

This impressed Animal. "You never!"

"She did. And she made him apologise."

"What d'you do, Sister? Give him a smack?"

They were delighted by this, but I was embarrassed.

"Isn't he like your big boss, though? I mean he can't sack you or anything, can he?" Baz asked, choosing a tuna baguette.

"You can't sack nuns!" said Nesbitt. But then she looked uncertain. "You can't sack nuns can you, Sister?"

I said I wasn't sure.

What I was sure of was that convocation was going to be quite long and that there was probably going to have to be a little interview with Rev Mother quite soon.

"You're for the high jump!" Animal declared, cheerfully.

He's right, I expect.

And now I am late for the TV monitoring, so must hurry over to the retired sisters before something ghastly comes on. After that I must give some serious thought to my soul and ask the Lord to forgive my impulsiveness and my flippancy, my lack of submission, my pride, my temper and my disrespect for authority. But in all honesty, Emelda, I have to tell you that if he had been rude to Nesbitt before the cake had hit him, I hope I would have thrown it at him instead.

Quite a lot of prayer work to be done, then.

There is a deeper issue, of course. I trust your judgment on these matters, dear traveller. Do you agree with the Bishop? Am I distracted from my spiritual duties by the Shoppe? He may be right. Let's both pray for guidance in this and all else. Wish me luck for convocation.

Best wishes,
Sister B.

37
ART

Dear Wanderer,

I've had an extraordinary week because Rev
Mother gave me a little holiday. After the Bishop
incident, she felt I needed a break. She looked in
the diary and found I hadn't been away from the
convent for more than a few hours for nearly twelve
years. It's true! When she asked what I would like to
do, it was easy. I said I would like to spend a couple
of days in Cambridge, if the Carmelites could spare
me a room, and visit the Fitzwilliam Museum. I'd
never been.

It was organised in no time. Nesbitt offered to
run the Shoppe and Alphonsus, who happened by
on website business, even offered me a lift. I was
surprised to see Hermione sitting in the car when I
climbed in.

Alphonsus' car is so different from the van.
It smells of mint and is a squat little thing, with a
throaty engine. Hermione didn't really have a seat –
she was folded onto a ledge in the back – but she

seemed happy enough. We were alarmingly near to the ground as we whizzed along.

"I'm carrying out a little survey and Alph has offered to drive me," Hermione explained. "I hope you don't mind."

"What are you surveying?" I asked.

"The pasture. Do you remember the Poore Pasture? I showed you the little map."

I said, yes, I remembered.

"I thought I might see if I could find it. I hope you don't mind a detour."

I said a detour sounded fine.

We drove to the outskirts of the city and following Hermione's instructions pulled off the main road into an area of glass and steel buildings with neatly trimmed lawns and trees.

"This is the Science Park. Is this where you meant?" Alphonsus asked.

"It's hard to say." Hermione was studying an old map, "This is the area, but it's changed so completely."

We drove around for some time. There were dozens of modern office buildings, widely spaced, with hedges and lawns in between.

"Is that sign any good?" I asked. We were approaching a large sign: a directory and plan of the whole Science Park.

We climbed out and held our old map up to the sign.

It was peaceful. Hearty rabbits were brazenly nibbling the grass all around. Science park life obviously suited them. The map showed a triangular field with its shortest side running along a lane. Ditches seemed to run down both the other two sides.

Hermione held the map up and rotated it in front of the sign. As she did the triangle suddenly matched one on the sign.

"Maybe that's it," she said.

The name on the sign was Genozome plc.

"Do you think the convent owns this land then?" asked Alphonsus, climbing back into the car.

"I'm not sure," said Hermione. "It's been rented out since 1868. The accounts list it every year. It's always described as 'the poore pasture' in the records."

We parked again and struggled out. A few people looked curiously out of their windows. They were probably wondering what a pair of religious sisters and a young man like Alphonsus were doing wandering about the Science Park. So was I.

Anyway, we crossed a road and passed a roundabout, and then Hermione stopped and said, "This is it. If you look carefully you can still see the shape of the field. A ditch there, another one there, and the lane where that cycle path is."

We looked at the map, and yes, it seemed to fit. It was a car park; trimmed hedging and paved pathways between rows and rows of parking spaces.

"Well, it's very nice," I said. "But what a pity, because it was worth something to us when people wanted to graze cattle on it. Only a tiny amount, obviously, but still."

Hermione looked at the rows of cars and then back at her map. "According to the papers I've found, we still own this land. I've checked very carefully and there's no record of a sale. We've only had one tenant all that time and it was Trinity College."

"That would be Trinity College who own the Science Park." Alphonsus said.

"What, they own this whole place?" Hermione asked.

"Have they put a big car park on our pasture without asking?" I asked. "That's a bit of a cheek."

"Without asking and without paying. As far as I can tell we haven't even had our three shillings a year for about thirty years." Hermione laughed. "I think they might owe us some money, actually."

"That would add up to about four pounds fifty in today's money," said Alphonsus. "I'm afraid that isn't going to build you a new tower.

We took a shortcut past the giant glass and steel building beyond the Poore Pasture part of the car park. It was very stylish and new. Smartly dressed people sat in the reception area, under a swirly mobile.

"I wonder what they do?" I said. Hermione pointed to a sign. It said "Genetic biomodelling for innovative medication systems". We weren't much the wiser, but it sounded impressive.

A burly security guard ambled over. "Well, sisters, what can I do for you?" he said.

"We were admiring your building," I said. "We think we might own a little bit of the car park."

"Oh, do you now?" he said. "Another chap was here yesterday saying the same thing!"

"Would he have been a small man, bald?" I asked him.

"Yes. Dog collar. Shifty. Didn't stay long."

"Mr Wooler!" Alphonsus and Hermione said at once.

"Would you mind, Hermione, if I showed these papers to someone?" Alphonsus asked as we walked away.

"Well, there's only one copy," Hermione said, anxiously.

"My Mum knows a bit about property. She'll take care of them, I promise."

So Hermione handed the will and the drawing over to Alphonsus and we all headed back towards the car.

I was at the Carmelites' lovely little guesthouse by lunchtime and in the museum before you could say "Post Impressionist". For three whole days I gazed and gazed. I started at the top of the museum and worked my way down – a system I warmly recommend. Each day when they closed I walked very slowly back to the Carmelites' house going over every treasure I had seen in my mind. On the last day I threw in a quick visit to King's College Chapel for the "Adoration of the Magi" and the fan vaulting and Kettle's Yard for the tranquility and the stones. My art batteries are now fully charged. I can last at least another twelve years, if necessary.

Your prayers are welcome, on the matter of the Poore Pasture, my soul, the future of St Winifreda's or anything else. And of course we send ours for your work and your lovely students and the workers making the orange peel boxes. We sold every one of them, and sixteen of the miniature llamas in six weeks – people love them. Considering what you achieved with the first installment, I imagine you will be planning your own King's College Chapel on the £163 I am enclosing. Try to find a local Rubens to do the altarpiece, if you can.

Best wishes,
Sister B.

38

MAGGOTS

Dear Emelda,

I was just wondering what can be done with our glut of swede this morning, when in came a lady with a lot of scarves. She bought some biscuits and instant coffee, and then began to scrutinise the swedes, walking round them and looking at them from different angles.

"Wow!" she said, "aren't they something?"

Well, of course I agreed they were, but I couldn't really make out what she had in mind.

She selected one and held it up, moving it round.

"Look at the colour, that amazing dusky purple and the soft earthy orange – and what would you call that? A bloom? That sort of dustiness, quite fabulous!"

So of course I looked at the vegetables anew, and you know they are very lovely.

"I'll take twenty-six of them," she declared. "I teach art at Lowfields Village College. They're perfect!"

Well, twenty-six swedes filled the back seat of her little car, but seeing them now with her eyes, I helped her to pile them in and gave her a discount in the name of Art.

And the gift she has left me is that every vegetable in the Shoppe now looks like an object of beauty. "Just look at the marvellous colour of these carrots," I said to Nesbitt.

"Yeah, right." she replied.

If only I could have preserved that buoyant feeling. Shortly afterwards Hermione came rushing into the Shoppe and said, "Oh, Sister B, it's too awful! You must come! I haven't told anyone, but you must come quickly."

She led me over to the old bathrooms near the kitchen where she pointed with a trembling finger, first to the floor and then to the light fitting above. I had to fiddle with my glasses, but eventually I could see a wriggling line of...maggots.

They squirmed across the floor into a corner one by one, as I watched. Then, following Hermione's trembling finger I tracked them back all the way across the floor and up into the lampshade, a transparent dish shape, which, on inspection, was teeming with them. There is something dreadfully unholy about maggots anyway, and maggots raining down from the light fitting made both of us shudder.

We struggled to think straight as we watched this little horror show, but in the end I realised that the maggots were falling through a hole in the ceiling around the light flex and tumbling into the light fitting from there. Then they crawled up the side and threw themselves over – presumably because the light bulb was switched on and made it too hot for them. They seemed able to fall their equivalent of a twenty-storey building with absolutely no harm at all, and trundle off into a cobwebby corner quite happily.

It followed that there must be something dead and full of maggots in the ceiling above the light and that something was very probably a rat, or perhaps several of them. Oh dear!

The pied piper of Three Fens, who came very promptly, is a large man called Wensley McHugh. His eyes don't quite agree. On his minibus its says, "Wensley McHugh Pest Controller rat's, mice and insect infestation's controlled fast and efficient". In my desperation I resisted talking to him about grammar or punctuation.

He approached the bathroom with the calm of a seasoned professional and examined the maggots. "That's come off a mouse, I'd say. That's a bit small for one off a rat."

There was a little comfort in that but, as I said, maggots of any size tumbling down on you in a bathroom are not very welcome.

"I seen worse," said Wensley, darkly. "I can sort it, but it'll have to be poison."

So now, Emelda, we are dotted with luminous green lumps of rat poison. We tried to avoid it, but blocking up all their holes just meant that the rats were walled inside the convent buildings with us where they starved slowly. At least with the poison they go quite fast. Wensley says they mostly choose to die in burrows, well away from owls. And we couldn't run the risk of rats in the kitchens, or worse still, the Shoppe or the pigpens. Imagine the fuss! No, we all agreed they had to go.

Best wishes,
Sister B.

39

THE TWINS

Dear Emelda,

How are your feet now? A pilgrimage is a challenge at any age, especially one that takes in part of the Andes. I am posting some special plasters from Boots (how appropriate!). They were recommended by Sergeant Tim, our local military man. He runs the Territorial Army group and marches them all over the place, and at weekends he passes his time by running over fells and tors.

He always runs to the Shoppe, which is how I knew all this, even though the barracks is nearly twelve miles away. The milk must be shaken to butter by the time it reaches his fridge, but he never complains. Anyway, these plasters are recommended by the professionals and can keep whole armies marching when otherwise they would be lying by the side of the road groaning, so I hope they work well over the snowy passes.

In the parcel there is also some Kendal Mint Cake, which Sister Bridget says is the other thing people on mountain passes must have, and some *pan forte*, which is what the Piedmontese soldiers carried over the Alps, and according to Sister Annunziata they hardly even noticed the mountains, so super-charged were they by this strangely solid fruity cakey thing.

The sad news that I have to pass on is that we have lost both Sister Angelina and Sister Merce – they were gathered in on Tuesday and Wednesday last week. Nobody was quite sure of their age; they weren't entirely sure themselves because they were orphans. It was quite a story according to a woman from the adoption society who spoke at the memorial service.

They were found in an orange box on the doorstep of a boarding house in King's Cross. Tiny twins that nobody knew what to do with. The owner of the boarding house, so the story goes, thought the box contained her meat order and left it outside for most of the morning before some passer-by noticed the newspaper twitching and heard a little cry. When they peered in and found not one but two orphan babies, they called a policeman who put the box under his arm and took it on the bus to St Thomas's. All this was in about 1907.

They joined us here in St Winifreda's in 1954 having already served long careers in teaching – they were quite expert mathematicians. While they were here both completed many more studies through the Open University. Sister Merce ended up with a PhD in Maths and her twin branched out and took one in Astronomy. We often saw her in the garden with her telescope. Perhaps just as much to the point, they were tireless teachers and ran evening classes at the Village College until very recently – we welcomed a lot of their former students, some quite elderly, to the service. It was a very joyful occasion.

Both the sisters had willed their bodies to medical science – which in their case means lovely Dr Greengross. They were part of his medical research project, and they loved his visits. Twin nuns are gold dust to the geneticist, as he said at the funeral.

It was a lovely address: "I am an old Jew and a scientist, the motives of Christian women who devote their lives to celibacy and prayer are beyond me," he said, "but I count many years of contact with Angelina and Merce as one of the greatest treasures of my life. They were generous in every way. They were funny and they were utterly good. They gave away everything they had. Not just things or money, but their time, their learning and even their blood for my study. People all over the world have already benefited from the discoveries this long-term study has produced. They will continue to do so. Goodbye dear twins, I will miss your holy laughter and I will miss your hand-knitted socks. One pair a year for thirty-seven years. I have been truly blessed!"

We kept up the tradition of tolling the bell once for every year of their lives. There was some discussion as to whether we should toll the whole number for each twin, but on consideration we realised that, of course, they would want to be rung out together.

So yesterday I did a half-hour stint of tolling the old bell, and I was only one of several – it struck me as perfectly fitting that it is a little difficult to keep count as you pull the rope; they were more or less 103 and we rang the bell more or less 103 times.

Dear things, we will miss them, of course, but they are in heaven and their indomitable spirits are fixed in the fabric of this place, so they don't seem very far away.

Speaking of the fabric of the place, it was quite hard work tolling the old bell because the rope is frayed and the tower's beams creak away like old knuckles. Several times there was an avalanche of dust and a sudden thud from above. Our dear sisters tend to have such long lives that the requiem bell doesn't get much exercise. I should probably try going up and oiling it, but I feel a little hesitant after the refectory roof. Pavel is away and we can't ask the community service workers to do it; Ted would have a health and safety fit. Another little matter for prayer.

Time now to prepare the next lesson for my intermediate English class. I think we'll do polite requests with modals: "Could you pass me the salt, please?", a little spelling practice and whatever the verb tense is called that uses "have been" (I always forget its name). "What has he been doing?" "He has been cooking all morning."

"What has she been doing?" "She has been writing a letter when she should have been sweeping the Shoppe." Whoops! No, "should have been" is upper intermediate; you have to be quite advanced in English before you can express pointless regret over things left undone. Probably quicker just to do them.

We all send our very best wishes to you and your fellow pilgrims.

Love and blessings,
Sister B.

40

THE MARCIANOS

Dear Emelda,

The Fens come into their own at this time of year. The land has all been harrowed to dark brown corduroy and veils of mist hang on the silvery poplars in the distance. There are lapwings on the fields and they make strange, haunting calls at night. The wind, to be rather less poetic, can be a stiletto, though it's calm today.

I have been feeding our new ducks, Hetty, Betty and Bill. They were a gift from farmer Odge, who thought we might appreciate the eggs. And we do. They sell well, too. I don't know whether you've got to know any ducks, Emelda, but they're very agreeable characters. They love food best of all, but they also thoroughly enjoy rain and will sit cheerfully in a downpour as the chickens huddle and look out at them, depressed. Ducks are optimists; chickens always fear the worst. Pavel has taken a great shine to the new trio and often visits their run. They shout with delight when he arrives and run plumply over to sit by him, hoping for treats.

Now that the work is finished, Pavel has taken up residence in Pigpen 1, while Pigpens 2 and 3 are free for guests. The deal is that our generous builder is there rent free for a year, in return for all his hard labour. He is busy working for Odge, who's extending his real pigpens, so he's paid too. He can't resist doing our odd jobs and we can't resist plying him with cake – both are old habits now. His English is close to pre-intermediate already.

"Sister, this tall one, this one here with the ringing…"

"The bell tower?"

"Yes. He is not good condition. These bricks are crack, are broken. Will fall, you know. Is dangerous."

He's probably right. The tower fund currently stands at £305.24 – a very promising sum indeed – but not enough for scaffolding, or even the clamps that hold the scaffolding poles together, let alone the actual repair work.

On the bright side, however, business is brisk in Pigpens 2 and 3. Nancy and Ira Marciano from Florida have been here more than a week. They just can't resist our simplicity and our wonderful countryside, Nancy tells me. Most of our guests are very self-effacing. They come, sleep, eat their breakfast (or not, if lovely Sister Lakmini offers them cabbage and kippers as she did one day last week – Sri Lankan breakfasts being a little different from English ones) and are off to the bright lights of Bury St Edmunds or Wisbech.

But Nancy and Ira are making us their base as they tour East Anglia. Ira is an engineer and an inventor. He tried to describe some of his inventions to me yesterday in the Shoppe. One was a kind of luminous paint and another an identity tag for the big steel boxes that go on ships. Both are huge bestsellers and have made the Marcianos a fortune. They give most of their money away. They have a foundation in New York and a hospital in Chicago.

For millionaires, which I believe they are, they live a frugal life. They don't like extravagance, which is probably why they do like the convent. They are both elderly, but in a tanned and dentally perfect way that makes them hard to date precisely. Nancy has a great fancy for Llama Shortbread and buys some every morning as they set off sightseeing for the day. She calls the sisters "girls" – "…and how are my girls this morning?" I wasn't sure at first, but now I like it.

Sister Dymphna has taken a party to Lourdes this week. Always a treat for all concerned, though they'll certainly keep her busy. Last year one of the retired sisters – Mother Beatrice, I think it was – flew home with a party from Donegal by mistake. The police said it happened quite a lot; one elderly nun looking a lot like another in her passport photo. It was nearly a week before we realised, but no harm done.

We looked up your questions about the baby armadillo, by the way. According to the internet it needs minced grubs, ants and salad and you need to train it to forage by showing it how to root around for itself. Which is easier to read than to do, I imagine.

Good luck to you and to little Fundadura.

Best wishes,
Sister B.

41

THE BELL TOWER

Dear Triumphant Captain of the winning Los Santos
Netball Team,

We were delighted by the idea of your netball
championship. When the outlying villagers
joined in, did they know the rules? I imagine them
piling in without much regard for the niceties, but
perhaps you explained it all. Fascinating that they
speak languages almost unrecorded. We looked on
the Internet and wondered whether they wore those
nose sticks to play in; health and safety issues, we
thought, but then you have five different kinds of
poisonous spider to contend with, so your priorities
would be different!

Farmer Odge strode over this morning – for dog
biscuits and Battenburg as usual, I imagined, but
instead of taking them from the shelf he declared,
"For heaven's sake, Sister, I've called my friend
Gibbs to look at the tower. It's a risk to us all." He
waved a brick-sized chunk of crenelated stonework.
"Look! It was a yard from the Range Rover. That

could have been my head or yours, or God forbid, one of my dogs'.'"

The surveyor came quickly, and was dour-faced. He ordered barriers all round the tower leaving a twenty foot space for falling masonry.

"Don't ring the bell, either," he said. "The rope's rotten and the beam that holds the bell is too. The whole lot will be down before you can say 'hard hat'.'"

He pointed to the buildings closest to the tower.

"My report to the council will declare the tower in urgent need of repair and restoration. It's a listed building. They have the power to carry out the works and charge you for them. And this building" – he waved towards the chapel – "is not safe to be used until further notice. I am issuing a statutory notice."

"But that's our chapel," Rev Mother said.

"Too dangerous, I'm afraid. The tower could come down and straight through the roof."

At convocation we prayed for help. How could we manage without the chapel?

"We must be practical, sisters!" said Rev Mother. "We can pray anywhere – the parlour or the refectory would be fine, or we could try the old barn. Let's be creative!"

And we were feeling quite cheered by that when there came a strong fenland wind. It was one of those swirling, gusting winds that make the weather forecasters tell you to look on their website for warnings. The kind that sucks up farmers' topsoil and drops it on their neighbours' land.

Trees thrashed and Sister Carmella (who ignores all weather) had to tie her lashing veil on with a Cambridge United scarf someone left in the Shoppe. Ted took the Community Service workers home; too dangerous. Just as I was rescuing the Shoppe sign from the hedge, there came a most startling noise. A terrible creaking and crashing and a strangulated out-of-tune chime.

The sound went on for what seemed endless minutes and a thick dust cloud flew out and engulfed the whole convent.

The Lord had seen fit to blow the bell down there and then.

When we inspected we found the damage had been quite merciful. Most of the tower looks quite its normal self from the outside. The top part, however, the part with most of the battlements and gargoyles has fallen in. The bell, looking surprisingly whole, and most of the rubble fell straight downwards, through the rotten staircase. We can see it through the window lying on its side just inside the door.

At least the Bishop's office can plainly see what's needed. Mr Wooler visits soon with his plan for our financial future. Pray for his generosity! We count ourselves lucky to have the dear generous brothers of the diocese to turn to. Of course their funds are limited, but when it's really needed we can always rely on them.

He hasn't actually confirmed this, but we're assuming that the surveyor will be happy for us to use the chapel. The worst has already happened, so we're hoping it's safe now.

We haven't had a letter from you for some weeks now, Emelda. We're all praying that this just means you are too busy to write, or that one of your letters just got damp in a canoe. God bless.

Best wishes,
Sister B.

42

HONESTY BOX

Dear Emelda,

So sorry to hear you have not been well. We are sending a tonic favoured by Sister Gertrude, but the special leaf broth offered by the medicine woman has, we all hope, already done its work and you are back in the classroom by now.

It is quite a lot quieter around the convent since Wensley, the rat man, set about his extermination. We did not employ him lightly, because we do believe that even vermin are God's creatures, but quite frankly they took advantage of this and we were overrun. This week for the first time in a couple of months, we heard silence in the night instead of what sounded like five-a-side rat teams playing their way through a league table on the rafters overhead.

The cunning creatures love walnuts and steal them from our big old tree. It is a good fifty feet from any of the convent buildings and yet we found nutshells all over the roof space. They must be extraordinarily well organised and determined to move them – it's the equivalent of me pushing a Volkswagen. We really admire their indomitable ways, but they had to go.

The Shoppe has had a bonanza this week, brought on by farmer Odge harvesting the giant fragrant field of leeks right across the road. His tireless team of labourers were all within a quick dash of refreshment whenever they had a break, and dash they did. We sold them piles of sandwiches and endless slabs of bread pudding, something they very much favour. It is hard and obviously very demanding work.

Feeling a little sorry for them running up and down the lane, Nesbitt, Hermione and I thought of loading our little handcart with their favourites and wheeling it up towards them. We piled it high, but then discovered the lane has a lot more of an incline to it than you might think. Using all our efforts we could barely shift it past the bell tower.

Soon we were blocking the lane and generally making a nuisance of ourselves. The rubbish collection lorry couldn't get by and we were beginning to think we would have to give up our little meals-on-wheels idea. Luckily a gang of the hungry workers then appeared and whisked us up to the main road. There were rewarded with bonus bread pud and we soon stationed the cart just at the turning.

All I had to do was put a little box on it for the money and keep it stocked up with fieldworkers' favourites and we had a very handy new little trading post. Later I put some eggs and chrysanthemums on it too; it looked a picture.

We've operated for years on the honesty box principle at St Winifreda's, so I left the little tin box on the cart without a second thought, but it wasn't half an hour before Constable Carl, the community officer, puffed up on his bicycle and told me it wasn't a good idea. He recited a long list of local honesty boxes that had been made off with and told grim tales of thieves who rolled up with bolt-cutters and spirited away anything that wasn't concreted in and kept under constant CCTV surveillance.

I said we'd pray on it, which threw him into twitchy confusion, so I offered him some bread pudding. To tell you the honest truth I was also hoping to distract him from the van; it is an MOT failure waiting to happen, and anyone with a bit of training could certainly find something about it to charge us with. Luckily his shoulder radio started issuing orders and he was called off to an incident in Waddenham – a good half-hour's pedal away. Bless him, he is an earnest, large young man and something about the uniform and especially the anti-stab waistcoat bristling with hi tech communications devices makes everyone want to giggle. We all remember him from primary school, which never helps.

Alphonsus walked by with a barrow of seed compost as we were talking.

"I recognise him," said the constable. "That's Dunn. What's he doing here?"

"Community Service," I told him.

Constable Carl sniffed and narrowed his eyes. "You don't let him anywhere near your website, I hope," he said.

I was noncommittal.

"Just don't go giving him your bank details or anything," warned the officer, and pedalled off to fight crime in the Fens.

The minibus needs a new tax disc next week, and we have just about found enough money to buy one, so I will pick it up when I do the next outpatients run on Monday. It began sounding very throaty when I was delivering veg yesterday, and I fear for its exhaust. We're all very hard at work with prayer for it.

It's been mild here and our garden seems confused. There are roses still flowering along the south wall – in November! We always have chrysanthemums, but this year we have a tremendous crop, and they are lovely golden things. We have bunches all round the convent, and I have sold armfuls to several village ladies who are taking part in a regional WI flower arranging competition.

I wasn't sure whether it was my duty to tell each lady that she was buying the same flowers as everyone else – there will certainly be a lot of golden chrysanthemum in their entries – but perhaps that won't matter. Sister Marcia would know, she's had a lot of Golds and Silver Gilts in her time, but she's in Turkey helping earthquake victims.

The mention of which makes me realise how small all our concerns really are. I only trouble you with them because I know you always like all our detail – the warp and weft of convent life, I remember you calling it.

I will also enclose copies of *Great Expectations* and *A Field Guide to the Animals of Africa and Madagascar*. Between them, these two books have been voted Best Ever Reading During an Illness by the sisters of St Winifreda's. The *Field Guide* is the most cheering thing you can imagine. My absolute favourite is the attempt to capture the animals' sounds in writing: "Utterance: short repeated barks, *yuark yuark*, frequently followed by grunts, *hurmm ummuh*, particularly when surprised."

That would make anyone feel better!

Get well soon.

Best wishes from us all,

Sister B.

43

LAND

Dear Emelda,

A burly man with a clipboard strode into the Shoppe this morning and announced that he was Graham Fulbright of Fulbright and Ricks. I welcomed him, naturally.

"Estate agents," he explained.

"Are we expecting you, Graham?" I asked.

"Yes, I'm due to meet…"

At this point Mr Wooler, our diocesan financial expert, sprinted in.

"Graham!" he cried. "You're a little early. Don't worry, Sister, this is diocese business. This way, Graham."

He bore Mr Fulbright and his clipboard rather forcefully out of the Shoppe and some distance away. They were soon joined by Roger Collis, and for the rest of the morning I could see them wandering all round the convent buildings. They took photographs.

When Rev Mother appeared, she watched them too.

"Why would the diocese or Intermediax be sending an estate agent to look at the convent?" I wondered.

"I can't imagine," she said. "I'll ask."

I watched her walk towards them. All three gave her rather nervous smiles. They left very soon afterwards.

At convocation Rev Mother announced that Intermediax wanted to buy some of our land.

"They have been very successful lately and they want to expand," she told us. "They need more parking spaces and possibly even a new building. They are considering making the diocese an offer for the three acres nearest the road. The meadow that is effectively our front garden. The diocese is all in favour. It would not affect our lives very greatly. We would still have the seventeen acres behind our buildings, where the kitchen garden and the orchard are. It would really just move us back from the road a little. Intermediax will pay for a new fence and have offered to re-surface our lane. They will be having very modern computers and we can have some of their old ones, if we like."

"But the meadow is where the sisters are buried." Eustacia pointed out.

"Is it? I didn't know that," said Rev Mother. She was shocked.

"Well you haven't been here long and the twins didn't follow the usual pattern because they donated their bodies to Dr Greengross. How could you know?" Eustacia said. "We've put all our sisters there since 1896. We don't mark their graves, but that's where we're all going to end up! It's our garden of rest."

Rev Mother blinked. She looked round at us. "What I need to explain, perhaps, is that the money Intermediax would offer would be enough for a lot of repairs. It would keep us solvent for quite a while. We could, for example, repair the bell tower properly and re-open the dormitories. Sisters, it would solve many of our difficulties, at least for the time being."

"But our sisters are buried there, Rev Mother," Eustacia repeated, patiently.

"Oh, dear me," Rev Mother said. "I had no idea. None at all."

"We can just explain it to Inter-thingy," Eustacia said. "It's easy enough."

"No, it's not as easy as that, because..." Rev Mother trailed off. "...I'm afraid I've agreed."

"Without bringing it to convocation?" said Eustacia, astonished.

"They told me they needed a quick decision. I signed something." Rev Mother put her hand over her mouth. She gathered herself a little and finally said, "We will offer this up in prayer and meditation. We'll soon know what to do. There's always a way, sisters. Always a way. There is one other thing."

"Is it the minibus?" I asked, my conscience showing.

"No," said Rev Mother. "It's about me. I've been offered a leadership position at the Cathedral.

The responsibilities are on a much larger scale. It includes a school and I would be in charge of religious houses all over Europe."

My head did an internal Munch scream, but we were all silent for a moment. Then I said, "Of course, if somewhere else needs you more. It's only right. And a school. That would be a great challenge and very valuable work." The words sort of hung in the air.

"It isn't decided. Not yet. I'm thinking it over, but I felt that everyone had to be told."

She fidgeted absent-mindedly with her rosary. "And there is something else, too," she continued. "I might as well tell you that even if we sell the meadow, Mr Wooler feels there is a lot of doubt about the future of St Winifreda's. The fabric of the buildings is beyond repair."

"Oh, it's not as bad as that is it?" I suggested. "A few leaks and a bit of damp?"

Rev Mother shook her head. "The bell tower is badly damaged, most of the North wing is unfit for human habitation, there are no foundations and the drains are beginning to collapse. The roof needs replacing – I know we've mended it with the help of the Pavel, but that's just a patch. What's really needed is a complete restoration and it would cost thousands and thousands of pounds."

"But we've been here for three hundred years," someone reminded her.

"Yes, and our sisters have always lived on a shoestring. In the old days parishioners were generous, the Church was generous, but even then, you can tell by looking that nobody had enough means to look after the place, except by their love and devoted daily work. I think we may be reaching the end of the convent's natural life. Devotion alone will not keep it standing, and sooner or later there will be an accident. I really fear it. Or we will just run slowly down. People will leave, we will…atrophy. Our work, our usefulness, will just end. It may be that there is no place for a community like ours in the modern world. Perhaps we need to work in different ways. We must be realistic."

Nobody could think of anything to say, at first, but then it occurred to me: "What will happen to the retired sisters? Where will they go? The rest of us could probably find somewhere, but they have been here for long lifetimes in some cases."

"There are places, Boniface. Retirement homes. There's one in the village."

"But it's not for religious sisters."

"No, but perhaps that wouldn't matter so much. Father Humbert could still visit them."

She didn't seem very convinced. We all gazed at the floor and tried to imagine the Ursulines displaced into Holmeview, the retirement complex in the village. No chapel. No shared prayers. No convocation.

"Perhaps they would enjoy the change. They are spirited women, after all," Rev Mother added.

But we knew it wasn't so. They'd had eighty or more years to leave the order if they had wanted to, but they hadn't. Theirs were lifelong vocations. Like the Queen's.

"They don't even have a TV rota," I sighed. For some reason this made everyone smile.

"You always cheer us up, Boniface. Thank you for that. We'll talk more about this, and we'll keep praying. It is all God's will, as you know."

(Strong language warning, Emelda. I know you're a woman of the world and a stouthearted one, so I give it to you verbatim.)

"God's will? God's will, bollocks!" cried Eustacia. "Why should we believe it's God's will to sell our sisters' graves for a car park just because you say so? They've gone and snaffled you! You've been offered a plum job to get you out of the way, so the diocese can sell the land and close us down. We're just a bunch of inconvenient old nuns living in a falling-down ruin to them. What do they care that fat cats will be parking their Porsches on our dead sisters' bones? The diocese sent you here because they could see you were full of ideas and they wanted to hide you away in a quiet backwater, but you were too clever. You made all sorts of improvements; you set us off in the right direction. We can be viable here, thanks to you. We can! We have our own electricity, our own water, the bed and breakfasts, the Shoppe. It can work, you know it can, but only if you stay and work with us. That's why they want you out of here to sit in Norwich in a cosy office. European responsibilities indeed! They can go and boil their heads!"

I don't know about the other sisters, but between you and me, Emelda, I quite enjoyed a momentary vision of Mr Wooler bending over a cauldron and carefully removing his spectacles before plunging his shiny bald head into the steam. GFM!

So that was convocation. We have all resolved not to speak of it again until we have had a chance to meditate.

I won't end on such an unsettling note. On the bright side, Bob Fairbrother has just bought sixty of the little boxes you sent from your villagers' work-shop. He is using them in his latest marketing campaign. The profits can all go towards your wonderful work at the mission.

Our thoughts are always with you, even if I do ramble on about our problems here sometimes. I hope you will forgive your correspondent and remember poor floundering St Winifreda in the Fen in your prayers.

Best wishes,
Sister B.

44

THE ONLINE SHOPPE

Dear Emelda,

Every spare moment this week has found me pondering possible reasons the Almighty could have for wanting St Winifreda-in-the-Fen to close. If it is His will, we must completely accept it, submit and move on with the lives He has planned for us. If, on the other hand, it is a test, a challenge, a kick up the backside (as Eustacia would put it), we must rally and find some way to keep going.

Last night, Mother Hilda, who represents the retired sisters at convocation and who quite often rests her eyes during proceedings, amazed us all by declaring that we should sell the meadow without a second thought. "It's the only way," she declared.

"But what about the burial ground?" we all asked.

"Oh, what does that matter? Our dear departed sisters wouldn't care – they've no need of those old bones, they're in heaven! They'd want the best for the convent, of course they would. No, my only doubt would be what those businessmen would want next.

If they've bought the front garden, what's to stop them planning to buy up the whole place? We've a lovely lot of land here, good land, nice and dry and well placed. That old Intermediax, or whatever it's called, will be having their eyes on the whole lot, I'll bet. They'll pull all the old buildings down and build themselves something fancy instead. They're probably already making plans."

I said, "Nobody can pull the convent down, we're a listed building."

"Ah, that never stops them!" said Hilda. "If a place is too far gone, they can get permission to finish it off. And if they can't get permission someone just drives a tractor through a wall. It goes on all the time. My brother's a builder. And this place is in a bad state, now, isn't it? We have to face facts."

I keep thinking we have fallen short of our ideals in so many ways. We have not been as aloof from the world as we might have been. I have not taxed the minibus on time twice now and the exhaust may not meet MOT standards. Actually it is held on with wire in a way that is perfectly legal in many countries, Pavel assured me, but may not be here. I also kept that three pounds that was left in the Shoppe in April! I didn't know whose it was, so I just put it in the bell tower fund. GFM.

But in Shoppe keeping, as in teaching, the show must go on. Alphonsus came in this afternoon to buy rocket and dolcelatte ciabatta and he waved his little computer about the Shoppe while I wrapped it.

"Just checking the Broadband signal," he explained. "We're wireless now, Sister B! Look!" And he showed me a picture of St Winifreda's – a rather lovely picture, actually, with the words "Home", "Convent Shoppe", "History" and "Pigpens B&B" along the top. It's the website.

"If you would like to give me a list of some of your stock and prices, I can put them into the online store," he explained.

"Do you mean runner beans and onions?" I asked.

"Well, you *could* put them on, but I was thinking more these little things the nuns make." He waved in the direction of the "Handmade Gifts" shelves tucked away rather inconspicuously at the back. "They could easily be sent by post. People all over the world will look at St Winifreda's website and they might order something. I've set it up so that they can pay online and you will get an email telling you what to post where. You just need to wrap it up and take it to the Post Office."

It had never occurred to me that there might be a worldwide market for pegs dressed as nuns, pipe-cleaner priests, bookmarks or holy doilies. It was astonishing. There and then Alphonsus photographed them with his tiny phone camera and before my eyes he somehow put the photos on the website. The prices I suggested he instantly tripled and he added "Plus postage on orders under £20".

It was all very impressive, but I'm afraid I still have only modest expectations for this part of the

Shoppe's venture. If very few people from the Three Fens area, people who know us and support the convent, want pegs dressed as nuns or piper-cleaner priests, what on earth makes Alphonsus imagine someone in Kansas or Montevideo might fancy them? Nice of the young man to try, anyway.

"Right," Alphonsus went on, "the last thing I need is the convent's bank account details. I can set up an automatic system, so people can pay online and the money goes straight in. I just need the details."

I hesitated.

"Don't you have them?" he asked.

I said, "No, it's not that." I was embarrassed. "It's just that Constable Carl told me not to give you any information about the bank account. Sorry."

The poor boy's face fell. "Oh, I see," he said. "Well, I get his point, I suppose." And he left. He even forgot his lunch.

"If you don't mind my saying so, Sister, you seem a little depressed," Bob Fairbrother remarked when he came for his walnut cakes later on. "You're very upbeat, usually. Is it the tower getting you down?"

"I'm afraid the future may not be too good for us," I told him. "It's all the buildings, not just the tower. They're expensive to repair and we really don't have much income. It's even possible we may have to close the convent altogether."

"Oh, my word, that's very bad news. How long has the convent been here, Sister?"

"Three hundred years," I told him.

He thought for a moment. "I could draw you up a marketing plan, if it's any use," he said. "I'd hate to lose the Shoppe. Your coffee and walnut is the reason my trainees always give me five stars."

For some reason, Emelda, I found this enormously cheering.

"What would your marketing plan do?" I asked. "I'm not sure I really understand what it means."

"Well," he said, "instead of explaining – I have cake here waiting to be eaten – why don't you come to one of my seminars?"

So I did. I took my notebook and my mauve Fenbiz pen and I attended "Fairbrother's Five Steps to Successful Marketing". And I took the five steps, so now we have a plan. It is humble enough, but it is a plan I understand. I won't give you too many details, but biscuits and nunpegs both play their part, and so do tiny boxes made of orange skins.

I was only half a day into the Five Steps when I realised how very much we would be needing Alphonsus Dunn. How could we earn enough to prop the buildings up and mend the minibus if we didn't even trust our website designer? At lunchtime I found him in the greenhouse pricking out winter salads.

"Alphonsus, I'm on a course. It's about online marketing," I told him.

"Good idea," he said, lifting a tiny plant into its pot.

"I've been unfair. I wouldn't give you the bank account details because…"

"No," he said. "You were right. I have a criminal record."

"I don't know what you did," I told him. "I thought you might Trojan the White House."

"You've been reading the *Daily Mail* again, haven't you?" he remarked.

"No, it was *What Computer*. Anyway, I wanted to say that…"

"Everything alright?" Ted's head appeared round the door.

I said, "I just wanted a quick word."

"Fine by me," said Ted, "but he needs to work at the same time or I can't count the hour."

So Alphonsus told me the story as he planted the seedlings.

"Look," he said, "you need to know what I did. How I got here. It was the Inland Revenue. I hacked the Inland Revenue – you know what hacking is? Right. Well I worked for an agency after I left university and they employed a lot of us techies to work on a contract for the Revenue. They were cowboys. They paid us as little as they could get away with and they charged the Revenue a lot – millions. We had to sign all sorts of disclaimers and official secrets and it was all to stop us from telling anyone what a rubbish system it was. Every corner was cut, it was all done on the cheap and the worst thing about it was the security. It was no good. It was easy to break into the system and look at other people's records – or change them even. It was easy to get it to send you a cheque. It's hard getting work at the moment, especially when you're just out of uni. We needed the work, but we all knew it was a bad, bad system; insecure, unreliable and way too expensive. The tax-payers were being robbed."

He tapped a seed tray and moved on to the next row.

"So, anyway I decided to see if I could hack into the system. I thought I'd do it and then tell my boss and the contractors and they would see how insecure the system was and change it. But they didn't; they arrested me. They charged me with breach of official secrets and fraud, they threw the book at me. I thought I was going to jail, but the judge, when he heard it all, agreed with me, more or less. I was convicted, but only of the lesser charges and that's why I'm here planting pak choi."

"Wasn't there some money involved, though?" I asked.

"Yes. I got the revenue's system to pay me a refund. I knew that unless I had something on paper to show everyone, they would just cover it up and pretend it hadn't happened." He dusted the compost off his hands and pulled out a wallet from his pocket. From inside he tugged a worn and folded piece of paper. It was an Inland Revenue cheque for 99p.

"You could have told it to give you a fortune!" I said.

"Yes, but I'm actually not a thief, Sister. Well, technically I am, but that wasn't my aim. It was a stupid thing to do. I was proved right, the system was scrapped and it wasted millions. But I have a criminal record now, and my chances of finding work in IT are about as good as yours are."

"And do you still want to do that sort of work?"

"Yes, I like it. I'm good at it. I've enjoyed making your website."

"It's a good one, isn't it?" I said. "I've been learning all it can do on the course. You did search engine optimisation on it and it's very good."

He laughed. "Yes, it's a good one."

So I gave him the bank details, and the online Shoppe went live (as we say in the business) last night.

Our bell tower may tumble, our gargoyles may crumble, but St Winifreda's coffee and walnut is here to stay – at least for the time being.

Best wishes,
Sister B.

45

A Visit to A and E

Dear Wanderer,

At convocation last night we agreed that each of us should take a retreat day and use it to quieten our thoughts so that the busyness of our daily efforts does not crowd out our real purpose. Mine will be next Wednesday, which coincides with the strike of the public sector workers, and although striking is a completely alien idea to us – and of course we have no pensions to worry about – I shall be dedicating my prayers to them and supporting their cause in spirit.

I had reason to be grateful to hospital workers in particular today because Sister Eustacia fell off a ladder in the top gallery while we were checking the rat poison last night. I was already in the loft space, peering about with a torch when I heard a resounding thud and a cry of pain. Very alarmed, I tiptoed along the rafters – we keep meaning to put boards down, but they're rather expensive – and looked down the hatch.

There the poor thing was, spread-eagled on the gallery. She soon sat up, but even from the loft I could see her ankle was swelling. The ladder had broken as it fell, so I couldn't get down. All we could do was call out, and since the gallery is a long way from the kitchen, the refectory and the chapel, we just had to wait for someone to pass. We said a few rosaries together.

Luckily it was Rev Mother who chanced by first and she swung into action, running to telephone an ambulance and sending Hermione to Odge for a ladder to fetch me down. I was soon out of the loft and accompanied Eustacia to A&E. The paramedics were called Rachel and Suze and you cannot imagine a more capable and genial pair of professionals. They are only young things, but you would trust them to cope with any sort of disaster. It really cheers the heart to think of such dependable young women standing by to rescue all the fallers and crashers. They wear green overalls and big boots and they can lift a nun on a stretcher, even one of Eustacia's build, without a second thought. We "blue lighted" it to Addenbrooke's in the twinkling of an eye.

Once at A&E we waited with the other casualties. It was a short wait, and I had nothing to read, so inevitably found myself speculating about what had brought the other people in. Some very obviously clutched a bandage or limped, some just sat looking pale and others came in big worried families and it was hard to tell who the patient was. Of course they were glancing at us, too.

A very polite man in a turban bought us both a cup of tea. A little girl called Amina showed me her bad knee and told me about her new bicycle. Then we were called and Eustacia was X-rayed and given a plaster – or its modern equivalent, which is a clever plastic shell with inflatable cushioning inside. The young doctor was Finnish, one nurse was Somali and the other was Turkish. What a treasure trove of worldwide medical talent! And all of them calm, kind and efficient and (I don't doubt) terribly over-worked and underpaid.

Thanks to the Lord for every one of them.

Blessing and good luck with the potholing – as if you didn't run enough risks without it!

Sister B.

46

INTERFAITH FESTIVAL

Dear Wanderer,

Eustacia is convalescing in Wales, which must be ideal, if a bit hilly for one in plaster. She wants me to pass on her thanks for the get well cards. In return I am enclosing a large bundle of Christmas cards from the sisters and many Shoppe customers too. We often tell them about your mission.

You asked for all news. Well, I have spent today at the Fenfields College Interfaith Festival. It was quite an experience. I arrived at the time agreed, but was at least an hour later than of any of the other stall-holders. We had been allocated spaces in the atrium concourse of the college in which to set up the stall.

Last year, Sister Agnes had rather a dispiriting time of it. She had taken what we think of as our travelling manger, which is a very beautiful little carved scene, but rather delicate and, well, small. She set it up on a trestle table and sat behind it and nobody really spoke to her all day. She told me she sat smiling and trying to look welcoming, but nothing seemed to help. Parades of young people of all descriptions passed by but absolutely none of them seemed to notice her. She sipped tea from her flask, she secretly said a rosary or two, and then it was time to go home.

So this year, determined to avoid a repeat, I took a huge new manger I made last week with the help of a few of the elderly sisters, and Sister Mary of Light, who is that wonderful thing – a trained primary school teacher. Nobody does crumpled tissue paper like a trained primary school teacher. And the elderly sisters are, many of them, highly skilled craftswomen. So let's just say that I sat this year in front of a life-size and unusually colourful Holy Family, a donkey that Disney would envy and an ox that Sister Mary of Light modelled on those fantastic musk oxen that we saw on *Frozen Planet* with wavy long-haired coats and horns like a middle parting with a lot of hairspray.

Of course it isn't a competition, but the Hindu stall was very attractive. They have the advantage, visually, with their great array of colourful gods. The one I could see most clearly was Vishnu, with four arms and a serpent headdress, standing on a lotus flower. Their whole stall was swathed in scarlet cloth, embroidered, tasselled and covered in tiny mirrors – and they burned incense. The effect was quite dazzling.

But this year I had an ace up my sleeve: giveaways. This strategy was Mr Hari Menon's advice. He happened into the Shoppe just as I was assembling the stall.

"Ah, Sister, you must draw them to your stall with a little treat!" he said. "A little sweet or a cake – it always works. Our greedy eyes and mouths lead us to the sensory pleasures and only later do the heart and mind follow."

I did momentarily wonder whether this was a strictly Christian approach, but then I thought, no, Hari is sent by the Lord and is endlessly wise and helpful with the Shoppe displays and the bookkeeping, so giveaways it would be. But what should they be?

Even I could see that few seventeen-year-olds were likely to be attracted by the only bite-sized item I had to hand – sprouts. So we asked Nesbitt.

"Flapjacks," she declared. "Got to be Flapjacks."

So flapjacks it was. Nesbitt baked them and I piled them, cut into inch cubes, in a pyramid. It worked like magic. The stall was busy all day. Hermione and I talked Christmas with a lovely variety of students and had fun trying to spot the type of course they were on from their appearance. Hair and Beauty was easy – they all had pillowy high-piled hair – and Uniformed Services wore a tee-shirt helpfully saying "Uniformed Services"; Performing Arts were dramatic and Fine Arts were artistic. Catering students examined the flapjack in a professional way for a moment before eating it!

The college is an enormous place. The art department had some great work on display. I went for an exploration at lunchtime and found sculptures made of elastic bands, and installations using masking tape and paperclips. Fascinating! I also found some leaflets about apprenticeships.

The boys favoured falling-down trousers and face-hiding hair. The girls seemed to have forgotten their skirts, but Hermione said those were leggings. I sold twenty-four packs of our very own hand-made Christmas cards and every single one of the pipe-cleaner priests and each and every customer found a tiny blessing written on the tissue paper wrapping their purchase.

Even the Buddhists were impressed!

Best wishes,
Sister B.

47

THE DIGGER

Dear Wanderer,

I have driven a digger! It is a monster; controlling it feels like riding a Tyrannosaurus rex. I was juddery with the bucket at first, but it wasn't too difficult and Geoff the driver shouted a few instructions, so after ten minutes I was scooping away at the ground and carving the long trench that will hold our ground source heat pump cables.

It was all because I happened by and stood watching Geoff at work for a few minutes, marvelling at the deftness with which he could make the great roaring, clanking thing take a bite of earth and swing it over on to the pile, and then go back for the next neat bite so quickly.

"Fancy a go, Sister?" he asked. "My mate's called in sick." He pointed at a second digger sitting idle.

I couldn't resist. I haven't spent such a delightfully productive afternoon in ages. We finished two trenches side by side and I was congratulated on my digger mastery, although I must admit the edges

I achieved were very rough compared to Geoff's. A surprising amount of mud and Fen clay flew up and stuck to me, but I was concentrating too hard to notice.

In the Shoppe, when I finally arrived, Nesbitt was cutting cake and three people from the council were looking round with clipboards. Nesbitt gave me a special look, but I couldn't work out what it meant.

"I believe you are the person in charge here," said one of the men.

I said I was. He looked me up and down with raised eyebrows.

"Environmental Health," he said. "You are selling quite a wide range of goods."

I said with some pride that yes, we were expanding and now we were selling cakes and sandwiches as well.

"Do you have a food hygiene certificate?" he asked.

"No. Do we need one?"

"You do. Strictly speaking you need one to be in force and on display at all times. Strictly speaking," he said, looking at me over the clipboard, "we could shut you down right now."

"Shut us down?"

"You need a special certificate you see, if you're preparing and selling food. We need to know that persons handling and selling food understand food hygiene. The consequences could be very serious otherwise."

"Oh dear," I said. "Have we broken the law? It was perfectly unawares."

"That is not a defense that will stand up in a court of law," he said severely.

"A court of law? Will we go to prison?" I asked.

"Hardly," he said. "What we would like to see is a valid certificate, that's all."

"How would we get this certificate?" I asked.

"In fact," he said, "it is quite a simple and straight-forward matter. An online course."

I looked at Nesbitt.

"You do it on the computer," she whispered. "You read things and then it asks questions and if you get them right, you know what you need to know and so you pass."

"Correct," said the inspector. "Anyone not able to do an online course can attend a training cen-tre, of course." He paused. "We're here purely in an advisory capacity, today. What we would like to see is a valid health certificate on the wall by the time we come back in about a month."

"You're not going to shut us down then?"

"No. In fact your hygiene practices here appear to be of a very high standard. I have spoken at length to your food preparation operative here," he nodded at Nesbitt, "and I have ascertained that she organises the sandwich preparation very profession-ally and is observing most of the good practice we would hope to see. That is very good, but for the protection of the public, you understand, a certifi-cate is needed."

So that was us warned. As soon as we had shut the Shoppe, Nesbitt and I went over to Sister Bernard's office and looked up on the internet to see what we needed to do next. Nesbitt was anxious.

"I hate things on computers, Sister," she said. "I really hate it. I can't make out the words."

Nesbitt never reads anything unless she absolutely has to and writes only the briefest of notes when it is impossible to avoid it.

"Perhaps we can do it together," I said. "I can help you with the reading and you can help me with the computer. We'll make one good 'un between us – as my old dad used to say."

And speaking of food hygiene, dear Wanderer, I was watching TV briefly last night while Mother Bernadette completed her last few dressed clothes pegs and I happened to see a programme about your nearest city up there in the high sierras. An electrician – a very nice man called Rex, had been sent there because it was the worst place in the world to be an electrician.

Rex was rising wonderfully to the challenge, trying to persuade the people of Lasanta that connecting their household equipment directly to the overhead power cables and slinging their naked wiring across the streets in sparking bundles wasn't a very good idea. At first they were suspicious of his namby-pamby First World ways, but soon they all realised that life without electrocution and sudden outbreaks of fire really was more fun, and then they all loved Rex and kept offering him big dinners and parties to thank him. The problem was their food. They favoured buckets of cow hooves, nicely boiled with lumps of fat. From two continents away it was disgusting; from the same room it was a far greater test of Rex's self-control than any amount of dangerous wiring.

"Here, Rex," they would say in subtitles, "try this piece of knuckle in a bit of kidney fat. We have saved this part just for you!"

I have included some digestion remedies with this letter. I'm not sure what they eat in your area, but I hope it isn't mostly cow hooves in buckets. I looked on the internet and it said, rather tactfully, that, "Hygiene is often questionable and you may quickly surpass your intestinal limits". Oh dear!

I'm off to study for my hygiene certificate, so that no-one's intestinal limits are tested in the Shoppe.

Best wishes,
Sister B.

48

THE CONDITIONAL

Dear Traveller,

I know how exhausting the heat can be, and the mosquitos must be dreadful, but three weeks of grey easterlies and deep snow have offered their own challenges here at St. Winifreda's. Thank the Lord the refectory roof, at least, is repaired, and the new boiler is boiling away – it makes a lovely quiet munching noise as it consumes its wood pellets. Even so it is bitter in the Shoppe and the roads have been very difficult, so custom has not been good.

The exception has been the migrant workers. Perhaps temperatures of -13 are nothing to young people from Poland and Lithuania, or perhaps they are just wonderfully cheery by nature! Who knows? But anyway, they stamp their way in, blowing on their fingers and buy extra cake and – a new addition to the service – my very own freshly brewed hot chocolate whenever they get a break from the picking and packing. Since many of them are also my language students, we use the opportunity for conversation practice.

Yesterday, having worked on conditionals in the lesson, they all carefully made their purchase in the conditional: "If I could have two convent crumble biscuits and a cake, I would be very happy, please, Sister."

"If it was available, a hot chocolate with two sugars, I would buy it."

One or two imperfections, but a pretty good performance on the whole.

Nesbitt is puzzled by this sort of language practice. "How come they're asking in that funny way?" she said.

I told her it was practice for the conditional.

"Conditional, what?" And when I explained, she said, "Oh, I could never do all that. I'm hopeless at English. Got a D. Hopeless."

And it was real despair, Emelda. She believes that she is stupid because she didn't pass this single exam, and yet she is as bright as a button. A hard-worker with great gifts. The Shoppe couldn't run without her these days.

So I said, "Nesbitt, Mr Menon thinks we should offer you some training, so you could get a qualification."

She avoided eye contact by repositioning the scoops in the dog biscuit bins for a while, and then she said, "I really hated all that stuff at school. I want to learn, but all the writing…"

"You did the health certificate easily enough," I pointed out.

"Yeah, because you did the reading part." She hunched her shoulders and put her hands into her overall pockets. "What I'd really like is to get paid for working here, but I know you haven't got any money or anything. And I'd really like to know how to make the cakes and things that French sister makes."

"Really?" I said. "It takes a long time – years I believe."

"I think I could do it. I can't cook properly yet, but I know how things go together. People like my sandwiches, don't they?"

And they do, they certainly do.

So I did two things. I rang Mr Highton at Fenfields College, who organises apprenticeships, and I spoke to Sister Clementine. There's paperwork, but by next month Nesbitt could formally be an apprentice. She will have to spend more time in the kitchen with Sister Clementine, she will have to go to college one day a week, and somehow we will have to find the money to pay her too. Apparently she could be sponsored; all we need to do is find someone willing to pay. We're already praying.

We have two brave hens who have laid right through the winter this year. We all feel great admiration for their doggedness in the face of snowdrifts and Arctic easterlies. Thanks to them we have been able to provide eggs every morning for the Pigpen guests. Nancy and Ira adore their eggs. They're still in Pigpen 2. They are a fixture.

"I don't just get an egg for breakfast, Sister. I get an egg from a hen I know by name! We couldn't even imagine such a thing back home, could we, Ira?"

"No, sir!" Ira confirmed.

"You girls are just the best! I'm right, aren't I, Ira?"

"You sure are," Ira agreed. "You bet!"

A satisfied customer is a fine thing. Why anyone should prefer the grey chill of Three Fens (icy, with fog and hail forecast for later), to the balmy warmth of Tampa, Florida (eighteen degrees today, I looked) remains a mystery, but we're very glad they do.

Best wishes,
Sister B.

49
MIASMA

Dear Sister Emelda,

It is hard to picture the steaming rainforest, despite your wonderful description. The nearest we come to the tropics here at St Winifreda-in-the-Fen at the moment is the miasma that has begun to haunt the convent's north courtyard. We think it might be drains, and have been praying for it to go away of its own accord for some weeks now. Yesterday a mysterious little fountain developed in one area too. We could, as Hermione remarked, just call it a miracle and invite pilgrims; it might be a natural spring. But to be honest it doesn't smell like one, so I'm afraid it will all lead to expense of some sort. It usually does. We soldier on!

The grim weather has actually boosted the veg sales. People stay in the warm and order by email. We have a little computer now in the kitchen, so I can take orders and keep an eye open for Pigpen bookings. Several new customers have signed up and as long as the minibus holds out, I deliver on a Monday while Nesbitt minds the Shoppe.

So yesterday I was pottering along Fen Drove at a very slow rate, the windscreen wipers not being able to cope with the hailstones, when I spotted, of all things, a runner battling his way along the road ahead. He seemed underdressed in only shorts and a vest and as I approached he stopped and very slowly folded down (it was too slow and graceful to be called collapsing) onto the wet roadside. I feared he would simply die of exposure left there, so I stopped and ran over with the blanket from the van.

Just as I was wondering whether I could lift him on my own, a car pulled up and with a soft *zzzub* the driver's window glided down. It was Roger Collis, of Intermediax.

"Trouble, Sister?" he asked.

I said, "Yes, he's collapsed. Can you help me lift him?"

Roger Collis recognised the runner immediately. "Oh," he said. "It's Jonathan from my office, he's training for the marathon."

We helped him into the car. By this time Jonathan was able to speak and was feeling quite embarrassed by all the fuss.

"I just became a little too cold. I underestimated the weather, I'm afraid," he said.

"You don't get this kind of weather in Kenya much, I guess," said Collis.

"No indeed. At home it is usually the heat one has to contend with," Jonathan told us, examining his glasses, which had been bent out of shape.

So that was that, really. Jonathan was whisked off to the warmth of the Intermediax offices and I went on with delivering the veg. But I did make a mental note to tell Sister Prudence that a fellow Kenyan was working nearby. I knew how keen she would be to meet him.

It was a long, chilly afternoon. I was back and shutting up the Shoppe when a man roared up on a motorbike. "Delivery for a Sister Boniface?" he asked, sticking his head in at the door. I signed for a box, but said I had not ordered anything.

"I just do the drop-off, love. You'd have to phone the number on the docket." he said, genially.

I opened it and found a shiny flat little mirror. The delivery note had the message, "Thanks for rescuing Jonathan, all at Intermediax".

After prayers I showed it to Sister Bernard, and was astonished at her reaction. She said, "Oh my Lord, Boniface! Oh Lord! Look, just *look*, he's given us an iPhone! Oh, I've wanted to see one of these for ages! I can hardly wait to…"

But then she pulled herself together and said, "I guess we'd better take it to convocation. They're quite expensive. Rev Mother might not want the expense of running it. You have to pay."

So we admired the little thing for a while longer, but then put it back in its box and went along to convocation. There wasn't time to discuss it immediately because we were still focusing on the miasma and the fountain. It seems a plumber is really needed now as the latest guests in the Pigpen Bed and Breakfast rooms have written, "Lovely room and delicious breakfast, but what's that odd smell? – Gary and Sue" in the visitors' book.

When I told Sister Prudence that a friendly Kenyan was working nearby she actually jumped for joy. "Praise the Lord!" she cried. "I hope he knows Nairobi! And I hope he will come to visit!"

It is hard being away from your own country, but we at the convent benefit enormously from our visitors. For one thing Sister Prudence's singing voice is a wonderful addition to our choir, and for another we are greatly cheered by her attitude to the miasma. Running a mission in the Nairobi slums gives you a wonderfully robust attitude to plumbing!

Best wishes,
Sister B.

50

STINGING NETTLES

Dear Sister Emelda,

My wrists are so sore from nettle stings that writing is a little awkward, but at least I can report that the mysterious fountain (how romantic that sounds – a lovely short story title) is mended. It turned out to be what Gareth the plumber politely calls foul water. There was a leak under the north court flowerbeds and, well, we won't bother with the details; it's mended and we are £210 down because it involved a lot of digging and a fair amount of new pipe.

But before any of that could happen the stinging nettles had to be cleared. "Nettles love foul water!" Gareth remarked cheerily, and went to sit in his van as nettle clearance is not a plumber's work. They were thick and strong and determined to stay, but I got the better of them in the end, with the Lord's help, even if they did leave my wrists raw.

The job fell to me because Pavel is away, Sister Bernard is on a course, Nesbitt is off on study leave and Carmella is behind with the vegetable planting because it's been too wet to garden for days on end. The weather has confused Sister Prudence. "In Kenya a drought is when there is no water," she remarked yesterday. "Here it rains all day and it is also called a drought – it makes no sense!"

Nesbitt has been doing famously well in her apprenticeship – Sister Clem is most rigorous – but Nesbitt is beginning to impress her. The only problem we have found is that Nesbitt must pass a level 2 English test. It's compulsory. I've been giving her instruction, but she is still paralysed with fear and the test is on Wednesday.

She doesn't know it, but she is almost definitely the most prayed-for candidate in the country since I mentioned her at convocation: two benedictions so far and a full mass dedicated on Sunday, and that's without the online prayer group, many hundreds strong. I'm very keenly hoping heaven agrees that Nesbitt needs at least a pass overall. If she can only remember a semi-colon and at least one set of inverted commas in the extended writing… Well, that and a few spellings, and using a capital letter for 'I' every time, and writing "a lot" as two words and watching out for "He should of told me", and… Oh dear…please do add a few prayers of your own – we might reach the tipping point.

I was in the Shoppe all over the weekend, hoping for enough custom to pay for the plumbing. The bestseller on Saturday and Sunday was Christmas Blessed Bunting, hand-crafted bunting with the added bonus of having been prayed over (one of Rev Mother's ideas). It flew off the shelves. Then there was a run on tea bags and chocolate biscuits. All in all it wasn't a bad weekend for trading. Even so, we were well under the £210 miasma money.

At convocation yesterday we offered up the iPhone issue for meditation. Sister Bernard, having done a lot of research, including hands-on use of Alphonsus Dunn's phone and a brief tutorial over at Intermediax with Belle, the receptionist, demonstrated some of the clever little thing's amazingly varied uses. It can take photographs as well as being a phone, and it can play music and send emails. It can even, if you point it at the sky at night, tell you which constellations you are looking at. It can. Seriously.

So we all listened and watched and marvelled, but despite all this it was difficult to see how it fitted into the religious life, except as a way of calling for help in an emergency. And, as Hilda pointed out, our Sisters had managed even in emergencies for three hundred years or so without one, calling for help in the old-fashioned, yelling-and-prayer, sort of way.

So it looks as if our gift will have to be returned, and it seems to be my job to do it, as I was the lucky recipient. Poor Sister Bernard handed it back to me very sadly.

Most of the language lessons are suspended for a while now, while my fieldworker students are hard at work picking leeks. I still see the beginners' class every evening, and we are using a very practical textbook called *Daily English*, which features jolly recordings of shop conversations and doctor's surgery dialogues and so on.

Today Nikkita, who is Lithuanian, had to ask Chen Li, who is Chinese, how to get across Middletown from the Post Office to the Cinema.

"Is go straight on, is left... No, is right!" They struggled for a long time, and both got the giggles so much that I'm not sure there was a lot of actual progress, but I felt somehow it was good for international relations. Besides, if either of them really did get lost in Middletown I'm pretty confident they'd manage perfectly well.

The doctor's surgery dialogue was also very revealing. It went:

Nikkita (as doctor): "Hello! What is problem?"

Chen Li (as patient): "Leg!"

Nikkita: "Leg? Is hurt? Is pain?"

Chen Li: "Ah yes! Pain. Bad."

Nikkita: "Take paracetamol. Goodbye."

Chen Li: "But leg bad!"

Nikkita: "Paracetamol. Goodbye."

I felt this revealed something about their NHS experiences. I was still raw from a brush with Conan the Receptionist (also known as Eileen Dumphries) at our local GP's surgery. "Paracetamol. Goodbye" just about sums Eileen's general stance towards the sick and needy, even if they happen to be nuns aged eighty-nine like Mother Maria Stella, who had fallen in chapel and banged her head on a pew.

We must pray for patience – our own and Eileen's.

Best wishes,
Sister B.

51

INTERMEDIAX

Dear Emelda,

An exhausting fortnight here because of a seminar at Intermediax. Smartly suited delegates from Sweden and Finland have been strolling into the Shoppe between sessions. I don't think they understand English pounds because they spent lots of them, handing over £20 notes without any of the little twitch local people undergo at the moment of release. They start at 8.30 am and finish at 10 pm, but there is time to buy cakes and even pipe-cleaner priests – they found these particularly amusing.

I feel I know a little more of the company since my visit there last week to return my gift phone. I made an appointment and went to see Roger Collis in his office. I had imagined the old outbuildings at Odge's farm to be rather a damp and humble place to do business from; they're behind a big barn so I'd never actually seen them. I was entirely wrong. They are all glass walls and indoor trees.

We walked past something called a "Gatherspace", which is where employees can, as Roger explained, "Just hang out and chew the fat creatively". It was empty – they had run out of fat or chewed enough of it perhaps.

So in his enormous office I explained about the phone, that we were grateful, but didn't think...etc. and he seemed really puzzled and said, "I see, I see."

And I said, "So we thought we had better give it back, but thank you very much all the same."

He said, "Why don't you just sell it? Keep the cash for good causes or building works, or whatever. No skin off my nose at all. Ebay."

I must have looked confused, so he said, "Leave it with me, Sister, I'll sort it out."

He leaned over his shiny bare desk. "I'm still waiting to hear about the sale of that piece of land, by the way. Any idea of what's causing the delay?"

"It's a cemetery. It's where the sisters are buried."

"Any coffees at all?" A glamorous lady popped her head round the door.

"Double Espresso for me, Carol. And for you, Sister?... Cappuccino, latte?"

"Cappuccino, please," I said, just to be polite.

"Nobody mentioned it was a cemetery," Collis went on.

"Nobody knew, probably." I took my courage in both hands. "Some of the sisters thought you might really want to buy the whole convent. Get rid of us. Close us down."

He was surprised. "Why would I want to do that?"

Our coffees arrived. Mine was enormous; a vase covered in thick foam.

"It's good land. You could build something really big," I said. "A huge glass headquarters."

He made a face. "No offence, Sister, but who'd want a corporate HQ in Hog Fen village? Naff idea. If I move to a corporate HQ it'll be somewhere with a bit more style. Cambridge. The Science Park." He leaned back in his enormous chair. "One of those ones with curves and an atrium. I want super-speed broadband and landscaped car parks. I don't want a crumbling convent surrounded by leeks and pigs."

"You could knock it down and start again," I said.

"It'd still be in Hog Fen. How's that address going to impress customers in California?"

This made us both laugh. I sipped the vast coffee. "The convent may own a bit of land in the Science Park, actually," I said.

"Well, lucky you. How come?"

"It was left to us in a will. We went to see it, but it was just a corner of a big car park."

"Could be worth a few bob, all the same," said Collis. "You should check it out. The thing is, Sister, we thought we were doing you a favour. We thought the convent was bust and desperate to sell that bit of land. That's what your Bishop's man…"

"Mr Wooler?"

"Yes. That was the impression he gave. More or less told us you wanted to sell up and close down. Offered us a low price for a quick sale on the meadow and hinted that there was already some other offer on the convent itself, so we needed to get in fast. Warehousing company I think it was."

"We don't know anything about that," I told him.

"Well, sorry, Sister, but Wooler isn't being straight with you. You need to talk to him."

"And what about the agreement Rev Mother signed?"

"I'll check," he said, "but it's probably nothing to worry about. Look, it doesn't matter what kind of deal they offer, there's no way I'll play any part in forcing you to sell. I'm not putting cars on a nuns' graveyard. It's a horrible idea. It would freak the customers out, especially the Italians. We'll use the verge like we did before, and I'll pay the going rate. OK? Now I should probably get on…"

"There's one more thing," I said. "You know you said you wanted to help us…"

"What next?" he asked, warily.

So I told him about apprenticeships. And by the time I had finished my cappuccino – which was nice, Emelda, in case you haven't tried one either, but nothing to get excited about – he had agreed in principle that the apprenticeship could work; his human resources people would look into it.

A few days later, into the Shoppe came lovely Brian from Intermediax accounts, always remembered as my first ever Shoppe customer, with a cheque.

Brian said, "Roger's spoken to the college and it's yes to sponsoring the apprenticeship thingy. This is the first payment. The rest can go directly into her account, if you send the details. Someone just needs to sign here."

I gave Brian a free Swiss Roll. I gave Nesbitt the cheque.

"What's this?" she said.

"Have a look!"

She unfolded it and frowned hard. "What's it for?"

"If you agree," I said, "it's your first pay cheque! You will be an apprentice of St Winifreda's catering department under the supervision of Sister Clementine, sponsored by Intermediax."

She stood in the Shoppe in her baggy brown overall and glared at the paper in her hands. "Bloody 'ell!" she finally said.

And now I know her first name too. It's Bluebell. It was on the cheque. Bluebell Nesbitt, our proper paid apprentice! (She would probably prefer us to keep that particular detail to ourselves, Emelda!) Oh, and she passed the level 2 test! No surprise to me, given her hard work and the heft of the prayer campaign. "Bloody 'ell!" she said again.

And all because poor Jonathan was blasted by the ill Fen winds.

Mysterious ways, as you know,

Best wishes,
Sister B.

52

REMAINS OF THE DAY

Dear Wanderer,

So many parts of the minibus have been replaced now that it's probably only the seats that are original. I said this to Sister Prudence, who crisply told me it would be considered practically new in Nairobi and would probably be in operation as a little bus, or *matatu*, bouncing along unmade roads and through traffic jams that have to be seen to be believed.

"You'd like Nairobi, Sister," she said. "If this were St Winifreda's in Kibera, you would paint 'God Loves Our Minibus' on the outside and keep praying. We don't worry too much about MOTs there! Any sort of working vehicle is like a dream to us. Many of my students walk seven miles to and from school each day. They think nothing of it."

What spirit! But poor Prudence is feeling the cold terribly, so we have diverted some money to Damart; just as important to keep the sisters moving as to keep the minibus on the road.

I have to close here as I still have to pack up the spectacles, cardigan and book that Father Humbert left behind when he called yesterday. Eustacia commented that the dear man would forget his head if it wasn't screwed on, but then regretted it when we all remembered that he is wearing a steel neck brace since the Seminarians' football tournament. The novel is *The Remains of the Day*.

"Who knew Father was an Ishiguru fan?" remarked Hermione.

There is another parcel for the post too: twenty-four decorated pegs, ordered and paid for by someone in Venlo. It's St Winifreda's first ever internet order!

Must rush, as not much of the day remains, actually,

Best wishes,
Sister B.

53

An Accident

Dear Holy Worker in Dangerous Places,

We have been reading about the kidnappings, the murders, and the drug cartels. Emelda, your work always takes you to places of risk, but this time you might be in real danger. The Embassy website, when we checked it last week, coded the neighbouring province red – "reconsider your travel plans". Which translated from Diplomatic language means "keep out". Is it wise to stay?

We've followed the official advice and our Response to Kidnap Policy is in place; it's in Sister Bernard's pink folder, but please don't do anything to put it to the test. For future reference, dear, we at St Winifreda's will speak to hostage-takers, because we will speak to anybody, but we will not pay a ransom, on principle, and obviously we haven't got any money either.

I have had an eventful week because of a mishap with the minibus. A huge straw bale fell off a lorry on the A10 and landed on the roof as I was coming back from delivering Lady Cottenham's veg box. The jolt and noise gave me such a shock that I steered off the side of the road and into a deep ditch. Firemen with cutting tools were needed. I am in one piece, but sadly the minibus is not.

The firemen made all the usual jokes.

"We thought you were going to a fancy-dress party!"

"That's enough of the effing and blinding, Sister – keep it clean, now."

They were brilliant. And the hospital was wonderful too. They sent me home after a week because, as Dr Susan put it, I had so many visitors that there wasn't really enough space to practice medicine in the ward any more. All doctors are sixteen these days, except the ones who are twelve, but very knowledgeable and kind.

So now I am home at St Winifreda's in the sick bay. The room has lovely views. Flat ones, obviously, but wide as wide. It's a full-time job keeping track of cloud activity. This morning, for example, there are Michelangelo fat, backlit cushiony ones – you expect a couple of putti and perhaps a robed and bearded Prophet – and in between there are delicate feathery, floaty ones, which might be cirrus. I'll ask someone to bring me a book soon, so I can look them up. In a couple of weeks I'll be able to get to the library myself, but not until they change the plasters. I can still type, but even that's slow.

Convocation comes to me, since I can't manage stairs in the wheelchair. All the sisters troop in every evening, so I heard the reading of the Bishop's letter.

FRAN SMITH

He thanked us for the hospitality but also said the structures of the Church were moving forward; the economic climate meant that there would have to be rationalisation; economies could not be avoided and many of these would perforce (perforce – his very word) have to apply in the area of the fabric of our institutional establishments.

Rev Mother was reading this aloud and looked up to see our expressions of confusion, ranging from slight to complete.

"He means the Church needs to save money on buildings."

"Ah!" we all said. "Quite right. Absolutely."

But then the Bishop went on. "I regret to tell you that in my opinion, and that of the Fabric and Structures Sub-diocesan Working Party, there can be very little place for outlying houses such as St Winifreda's in the Outline East Anglian Three-Year Episcopal Plan."

Eustacia grew impatient. "What in blue blazes is the man getting at?" she cried.

"Well there are six more paragraphs, but in a nut-shell he thinks we will have to close down," Rev Mother, said, abandoning the reading and rubbing her eyes.

It was the first time we'd actually heard it said out loud. Nobody could speak. We struggled to take it in. We asked a lot of questions, but there were no answers available. The Bishop simply doesn't think we can afford to go on.

"Well," said Rev Mother, "I imagine Hermione is now going to tell us that the convent has been receiving letters like this from the Bishop for the past three centuries."

"Yes, that's true," said Hermione. "They ignored them. Other times they scraped by with a little bequest or donation. Once or twice the Bishop died before he could take any action."

We prayed in silence for a while – I for one rather struggling to keep that last thought out of my mind.

"Well, sisters," Rev Mother finally said, "there is inspiration in the long struggles of our sister-hood over the years. Knowing that the convent has been told that there is 'very little place' for it in the Church's plans on and off for centuries, is, some-how, a great source of strength."

She sat up straight and beamed around at us. "We certainly need to pray on this. So much so that, really, I think it would be better not to discuss it any further. Now, I'm thinking about organising a conference: Helping the Poor When You're Poor Yourself. What do you think?"

We all had a lot of ideas. Yours would be most welcome too. I offered to type the agenda, because although I love a Fenland sky I am, to tell the truth, a little bored tucked away here in the sick bay and I'm longing for diversion. And having time on my hands doesn't help when it comes to worrying about the convent's future.

All prayers welcome, as usual,

Best wishes,
Sister B.

54

A Secret Love

Dear Wanderer,

What a flood of ideas! I'll pass them straight on to Rev Mother. She'll be delighted. I was impressed by #23: "Make shoes from old car tyres", but when I showed Sister Prudence, she said, "Oh, that is well known! I have a pair in my suitcase." She will be running a workshop you would like: Educational Materials from (Practically) Nothing. It's already fully booked.

Kind retired sisters keep dropping in and offering me needlework projects to help pass the time. How can I tell them I'd rather do almost anything than embroider or (even worse) crochet? Luckily, Hermione found me another challenge. She came in with a little wooden box yesterday. It's a pretty thing, about two feet by one, nicely inlaid, with brass hinges. Locked.

"A little bird told me you were good with locks," she said. "I've got down to the bottom of the pile of papers in the library now, and this is all that's left. I've looked everywhere for a key. I've asked all the sisters if anyone knows of the box or the key. Nobody does, so it's a little challenge for you. I've brought the toolbox. I thought you might prefer it to tapestry."

"I prefer torture to tapestry!" I said. "This will be fun."

And it was, but sadly not for very long; it was a very easy lock.

Inside the box was a single sheet of paper. It was a letter:

The Grange
Hog Fen
March, 1865

Mary, my dearest,
You will never read this nor understand the grief it gives me to see you, cheerful, holy, hard-working, innocent, contented in that place, when the life I yearn to offer you is so different. You have done nothing, nothing whatsoever to encourage my affections. I should never have kissed you, yet my heart can never regret it.

When my time on earth is ended I will bequeath to you this pretty box and, if it is within my means, I will leave also to the convent my treasured books and the only piece of land I own. It is little enough, but if it should serve to make life in any measure easier for you and your sisterhood, I will have achieved something.

I shall request also that this box and thus this letter remain in the convent near you.

It will comfort me to think of this box undisturbed on a shelf, quietly present, watching over you, as I myself cannot.

I ask for God's blessing upon you, and upon your most loving and devoted servant,

Robert Woodgate

"Robert Woodgate. He's the one who left us the Poore Pasture in his will," I said.

We looked at the curly handwriting. The wood inside the chest still had a fresh smell. "So this must be the chest he mentions," Hermione said. "He wanted it to stay in the convent library so it would be near her. He loved her and he wrote this to tell her without really telling her. That's very sad."

"Do you think she ever read the letter?" I wondered.

"The will asked them not to open the box," said Hermione.

"She might have been tempted," I said.

"She wasn't easily tempted, though, was she?" Hermione folded the letter again and put it back into the box. "He died, what, three years later, and he hadn't married because he only mentions his brother and his servants in the will."

We don't know who Mary was, exactly. There have always been many sisters with that name. There was certainly a Rev Mother called Mary at around that time, she lived to be seventy-eight. She seems to have been the one who wrote the little history of St Winifreda's that Hermione found among the papers.

I read the letter out at convocation, and a few tears were shed for the poor, sad pair – especially, I noticed, by Hermione.

"That girl needs to toughen up," remarked Eustacia, after she had left, clutching a tissue. "A couple of nights' television is what she needs."

"God forbid," said Rev Mother. "It was a sad little discovery, and very poetic, but I must admit I was rather hoping for a nice chest full of pearls or gold sovereigns."

"I nearly bought a lottery ticket yesterday," Mother Hilda confessed.

We all agreed that was definitely a step too far.

Now I must sign off so that Hermione can take this letter down to the post. And after prayers I will press on with the bookmark I am embroidering. I do it as a test of character. You, Emelda, probably skin rattlesnakes with your teeth as a test of character, but we can't all be pioneers!

Yours, determinedly,
Sister B.

55

THE BATTISHAM COACHMAN

Dear Emelda,

The sick bay window looks down the lane and I often see Ira Marciano, our Pigpen guest, on his afternoon cigar stroll. Several times now I have watched him, leaning on his stick, puffing little smoke signals whilst contemplating the tower. He looks like a thin little Churchill. On Monday he walked round it for most of the afternoon, scrutinising it from all angles.

He and Nancy often call in to the sick bay.

"I gotta say, Sister B, that's some crazy old tower you guys got there. I swear those monsters up the top are about to take off and fly right away. I took quite a shine to that tower."

"It's a bit of a worry, Ira," I said. "The whole thing's falling down, as you can see."

"A damned shame, I call that," he remarked, "if you'll excuse my French."

I agreed.

"Something should be done. It's history. As a matter of fact it's part of Nancy's history. We found out the old gal's family comes from right around here. Did some research. She has connections."

Nancy came in from the side room; she always insists on making me tea.

"What's that old fella telling you?" She laid out Armadillos on a plate.

"I was telling Sister B you got family here."

"I do! Turns out my grandfather came from Battisham."

I said, "Well, Nancy, you are a fenwoman!"

"I know! There're even kinsfolk left over there in the village. We met them in the pub. It was a great day, wasn't it, Ira?"

"You bet it was!" Ira agreed.

"I always wanted to find my family. My parents died young. Turns out my grandfather left Battisham in 1884. And do you know what he did? He was a coach-maker. A coach-maker!"

"I bet he made coaches that went right down this lane," Ira said. They stood beaming, side-by-side, looking out of the window.

"Right down this lane. Can you imagine! He could have looked up and seen this tower." Nancy took Ira's arm. "Come on, old fella, drink your tea. We got sightseeing planned."

Yesterday there was a Folly Towers Preservation Society coach trip and I watched as Ira, puffing on his cigar, got talking to whiskery Philip Downs. Even though the tower is fenced off, FTPS members still very kindly insist on coming and paying the full £5. They walk around the safety fence, pointing their cameras through the mesh, and seem quite satisfied with the arrangement. Nesbitt has extra cake ready; big slices to reward them for their loyalty.

I've heard quite a bit of radio since being laid up, Emelda, and one of the programmes recently was a medical one about tropical diseases. It is probably the equivalent of reading a medical encyclopaedia and then deciding you have most of the illnesses, but the things you can catch from South American rivers still haunt me. Parasites that do things you can't even contemplate without several Hail Marys. It was worse on the radio. I imagined what it all looked like; much worse than actually seeing. (Although God forbid I should ever actually see the maggot of Taniga Fruit Fly in action, either.) All this is leading up to the warning: if you or anyone else sees a little green fly land on them, please go and see a doctor straight away!

The get well cards now run all around the sick bay, all down the passage and halfway to the front parlour. Please thank your pupils very, very much. They cheer me every moment of the day. Special thanks to little Diego, who seems to have made four. He is at that lovely stage of drawing where people have a single hair – often long and winding – and no body, but lots of fingers!

Best wishes to you all – and please remember about the flies!

Sister B.

56

A New President

Dear Emelda,

Brilliant news that you have a doctor visiting now. I know I am squeamish about bites and stings, but that's just inexperience – or so Prudence tells me. A few years in the jungle and I'd get over it, apparently. Don't tell me any more stories about those snakes, though.

Rev Mother had a surprise announcement at convocation on Monday. It was about the tower. "The Folly Towers people want to sponsor the renovation of the tower," she told us.

"Sponsor?" asked Eustacia. "Sponsor in what sense?"

"In the sense of paying for it, I think."

"In return for…?"

"In return for putting up this plaque and something called a webcam." Rev Mother held aloft a neat brass plaque about the size of a hymnbook.

"What's a webcam?" we all asked Sister Bernard.

"A tiny camera that sends pictures over the internet. They want to be able to watch the renovation as it happens from anywhere in the world."

We were stumped by that.

"It happens quite a lot. On the internet you can see all sorts of things as they happen. For example, when Sister Clementine feels homesick she sometimes looks at the webcam that shows the Old Port in Marseilles. She likes to watch the fishermen unload their catch for the market."

"I don't want a camera spying on us day-in day-out!" said Eustacia.

"It won't. It will look directly away from the convent and focus on the tower. It won't be able to move."

"It seems a modest enough request to me," said Rev Mother. "The renovation will cost them many thousands of pounds and they want to help raise the money by allowing tower enthusiasts to watch. They have undertaken to employ top experts – many of them are FTPA members – and it won't cost us a penny. I think a web-thingy and small plaque are very small things to ask for in return."

All we have to do is write and agree, and the work will begin. We're having special prayers for thanks on Thursday.

When Nancy and Ira came for tea on Tuesday, I could hardly wait to tell them. They were pleased, but in rather a quiet way, I thought.

"Well that's nice, dear. We're just glad you don't need to worry about the tower any more," Nancy said.

"We're going to be leaving soon, Sister," Ira said. "We hate to go, but we have responsibilities back home, you know. The Foundation won't run itself."

I said, "Our favourite bed and breakfast guests leaving! What shall we do without you?"

"We'll miss the place too, dear," said Nancy, "but we certainly won't forget St Winifreda's, will we, Ira?"

"We sure won't," said Ira. "No way José!"

Nancy took a biscuit and passed one to Ira. Then she suddenly burst out, "Oh, Ira, honey, I just can't do it! I'm sorry, I just have to tell! I *have* to!"

"Oh, you go right along," Ira said. "You never could keep a secret."

"It's us!" Nancy said. "Ira met the tower man…"

"Philip," Ira prompted.

"Yes, Philip. And Philip told Ira about the Tower Society and Ira told Philip he really wanted to preserve the tower too, so they got together and they worked it out and to cut a long story short, Ira is the new President of the Folly Towers Association!"

"East Anglia Branch," said Ira.

"East Anglia Branch, and the Foundation has agreed to sponsor the tower as long as the work can be filmed and used to promote tower repairs all over the world!"

"I get to sit at home in Florida and watch your Polish guy do the work! Ain't that something?"

The pair of them were full of glee.

"And we'll be back, Sister B. Don't you worry. We want to see that thing good as new and hear that bell ring to celebrate!"

It will probably take five years. Parts of the tower need to be dismantled before they can be rebuilt, but when it's finished it will be a sound structure for the first time ever. God be praised!

I asked Ira why he especially wanted Pavel to work on the tower.

"Marciano's Law," he said. "Never let a good worker go."

I'll have to close now as the physiotherapist is coming to take me through my exercises. She disguises herself as an unexceptional little woman but, Emelda, beneath that mild exterior beats the heart of a tyrant. She makes me use muscles I never knew existed. Glutes, abs, pecs – she delves in and finds them all. Ninja Physio Unknots Nun! (Did I mention I've started reading the newspapers again?)

Best wishes,
Sister B.

57
A Meeting

Dear Wanderer,

Our plans for the Helping the Poor conference have really taken off. Conferences are Rev Mother's forte and she has a dozen workshops fully booked already. At convocation last night we agreed to extend it to two whole days and podcast some of it on the internet. We were just wrapping up when Hermione caught Rev Mother's eye.

"Yes, Hermione?"

"Err, one more thing…"

"Yes, Hermione."

"I've had a letter from Crabbe, Hawson and Dunne."

"And who are they?"

"Solicitors."

"Oh dear," Rev Mother said. "Is it something else to worry about?"

"No. Well, yes. I mean it depends what you mean… It's about the Poore Pasture."

Everyone said, "What?" so she had to explain to all the sisters about the little piece of land.

"The thing is, we thought we'd found it, so Alph – Alphonsus, told his mother. She's a solicitor and, as it turns out, a property law expert.

"Are they selling us? Will we be out on the streets?" cried Mother Hilda, who had just woken from a little doze.

"No, dear, she's helping us," I tried to explain.

"Mrs Dunn thinks we were wrong."

"We don't own any land, did she say?" Eustacia asked me.

Rev Mother said, "Sorry, Hermione, nobody's sure what you're talking about."

"Mrs Dunn thinks the Poor Pasture isn't the little piece of the car park we saw when we went there," Hermione explained. "She sent us a diagram. I've put it on a big sheet, so we can all see."

She pinned an enlargement of a section of map up on the wall. We all leaned forward.

Hermione pointed to a triangle outlined in green. "This is the car park, where we thought the Poore Pasture was."

It sat in the corner of a much larger triangle, outlined in red. "The red triangle is the land that Mrs Dunn's researches have shown to be the Poore Pasture."

"It's much bigger," Eustacia commented. "What's the black square?"

"That's a big office building. Mrs Dunn believes that the Poor Pasture now has a big office on it."

"What's the girl saying?" asked Mother Hilda. "What office building?"

"It's an oversight," Hermione went on, "a mistake, but St Winifreda's – we – still own a piece of the Science Park with a company called Genozome's head office on it."

"How did that happen?" Eustacia asked.

"Nobody's sure, but it looks as if Trinity College kept asking the convent to sell them the land – from the 1870s onward – but they couldn't persuade them. The sisters wouldn't sell. Then, when Trinity began to develop the Science Park, somehow their ownership of the land just came to be assumed. If we can show that we do still own the land, we might be able to negotiate for outstanding rent."

A long silence fell over our convocation.

"Might be able to?" asked Rev Mother, cautiously.

Hermione found her glasses and, jamming them onto her nose, read from the letter. "'In an unusual case such as this, the settlement would wholly depend on the parties negotiating a settlement.' They want us to send someone to a meeting on Tuesday."

Rev Mother said, "And the meeting on Tuesday is to...clarify?"

"Well, Mrs Dunn says it may be quite a long negotiation, but this would begin it. We would make our claim, so to speak, put it to the college, and see how their lawyers react."

"And would Mrs Dunn be willing to negotiate on our behalf?"

"Yes, she says she would. But she also says" – she frowned down at the letter again – "I would recommend that at least one representative of St Winifreda's be present, as this is a highly unusual set of circumstances."

"Well, I must say that is quite a responsibility," said Rev Mother. "It all sounds rather intimidating. Perhaps we should refer this to the Diocesan office."

Eustacia bridled at this. "The Diocesan office has washed its hands of us. Why ever should they be involved?"

"They have more expertise. They probably negotiate over property quite often. Someone like Mr Wooler would know exactly what to do."

"That would be 'sell off the meadow' Wooler, would it?" said Eustacia. "That would be 'close St Winifreda's and all other outlying houses' Wooler, would it? Or would it be 'economies must perforce be made' Wooler?"

"Eustacia! Do please try to be patient!"

"Forgive me, Reverend Mother, but I don't see why we, who have run this place for so long and have now, thanks to Hermione's ingenuity, found this piece of land, should not be quite capable of negotiating a settlement. We have the power of prayer on our side and besides, we do actually own the land. We have the law on our side too, do we not?"

"When I spoke to Mrs Dunn she did say a certain amount of diplomacy might be needed…"

Hermione said.

"Well, that lets me out. I'd be for knocking their heads together!" Eustacia said. "But you can do it, Rev Mother. You and Hermione."

"We need someone with a head for business, too, I think," said Rev Mother. "Boniface, would you come? If you can tear yourself away from your embroidery, that is!" She glanced at the squashed, knotted and unfinished piles of needlework around us.

Several of my sisters giggled at that, believe it or not.

And so it was that on Tuesday morning, Rev Mother, Hermione and I arrived at the lawyers' offices in Cambridge. It was a modern building with a lift for the wheelchair. It is not nice being in a wheelchair, I would not recommend it to anyone, but travelling in Tim the Taxi's special wheelchair cab and then being whisked up to the efficiently accessible boardroom was perfectly easy. We were there first and positioned ourselves around a vast shiny table. Picture windows gave views over the river, the spires of the city and clear, cold sky.

A smart young woman offered us coffee. We were too nervous.

Mrs Dunn was next to arrive; a small, vigorous woman in her sixties, in a plum-coloured suit and sharp spectacles.

"Morning, ladies. If you'll permit me, I will open the discussion and point out the case as we see it. We can only really throw ourselves on their mercies. We, that is to say, you, the convent, do have certain rights here, but your position isn't all that strong. Technically, they could claim to owe you very little. I don't think they will, but you can never be sure. Depends whether they send a lion or a wily diplomat."

"What will they say?" asked Rev Mother.

"Well, the college claims that on several occasions letters were sent to the convent seeking to buy the Poore Pasture."

"Yes, we have a number of such letters," said Hermione.

"The difficulty is that we are trying to prove a negative. They assert that the convent must have agreed to a sale at some point, it's up to us to prove that it did not. Leave the talking to me, at least at first."

The double doors flew open and in walked a very tall man in a widely pinstriped suit. He carried an elegant briefcase, which he threw onto the table before reaching across.

"Morning," he said. "Quentin Ryder, representing Trinity College."

He spoke only to Mrs Dunn, not even glancing at the rest of us.

"Marjory Dunn, representing St Winifreda's," said our solicitor, shaking the London barrister's hand. Cufflinks flashed.

"This is Reverend Mother Elizabeth Carpenter, Hermione Baxter, the convent's archivist and Sister Boniface."

"I'm surprised to see your clients present," said Ryder. He made no attempt to shake our hands and did not so much as glance in our direction.

"Are you objecting?" asked Mrs Dunn.

"Not in the least. I am merely surprised that the sisters – and so many of them – felt it worthwhile to attend what is a purely a very brief technical discussion."

"I felt it appropriate. Shall we make a start?" Mrs Dunn opened a file.

Ryder threw his briefcase open and extracted papers. He settled himself on a chair, uncapping a thick gold-nibbed fountain pen.

"Our contention is, and our documents solidly bear this out, that the land known as the Poore Pasture in King's Hedges was sold to the college in or around" – he glanced at his notes – "eighteen-ninety. We have letters to show that a sale was under discussion at a time when the convent was in need of funds and willing to dispose of the land by selling it to the long-term lessees, in this case Trinity. As such we feel the college is able to show good circumstantial evidence of ownership of the land and it is our contention that no claims against the college need be countenanced. Despite this, the college is willing to recognise the longstanding ownership the convent had of this land, and a very modest amount of outstanding rent, and make them an offer in charitable settlement."

"Would you be in a position to disclose the nature of that offer?" asked Mrs Dunn.

"The current ground rent stands at four hundred and twenty-five pounds. The college would be prepared to allow that sum to the convent," Ryder replied.

Mrs Dunn smiled very slightly. "That would be a one-off payment?"

"The college is prepared to allow the convent to continue to benefit from that ground rent."

"So, four hundred and twenty-five pounds a year." Mrs Dunn wrote this down, very slowly and carefully.

"Indeed," Ryder said, graciously nodding in our direction without actually making eye contact.

There was a pause. Ryder re-capped his pen.

"I wonder if you have seen this document?" asked Mrs Dunn, passing a printout across the table.

"This would be…?"

"This would be the estate agents' details of a property on the Science Park called Genozome House. Unit 206A."

"How does this concern us?" asked Ryder.

"On page two you will find what they call the executive summary," said Mrs Dunn. "It includes the expected annual rental income from Genozome House."

Ryder turned the page.

"The amount suggested is considerably more than four hundred and twenty-five pounds, I think."

"I fail to see—"

"The annual rental income from Genozome House is, I think it says, £1,459,690 and 88 pence."

Rev Mother gripped my arm. We all held our breath.

"The convent has no outright evidence of ownership of this land. The records on the convent's side are so poor as to be non-existent," Ryder said.

"Sorry, but that's not true," Hermione interrupted.

Ryder's head swung round and directed a searchlight stare at Hermione. Luckily she was fiddling with her papers and missed it.

"I had expected this to be a professional discussion," he said, turning back to Mrs Dunn.

"Miss Baxter is a trained archivist, she is perfectly qualified to express an opinion," Mrs Dunn replied.

"Nonetheless, I had hoped to keep this to the legal issues. As you well know, the expense of our discussions will increase very rapidly if we are distracted by—"

"Here!" said Hermione. "We found this!"

"Sorry?" said Ryder.

"It's a letter, a love letter."

"Now really…" said Ryder.

"It explains, I think, why the sisters would not sell the land."

"I have not been notified of this letter," said Ryder, straightening his shoulders.

Mrs Dunn slid a spare copy across the table towards him. He read it fiercely.

"You are contending then, that successive generations of your sisterhood refused to sell the land because of a romantic liaison…one that, as far as I can see, never amounted to anything."

"Mr Woodgate respected Sister Mary's calling and the sisterhood chose to respect the conditions of his bequest," Rev Mother said. "We kept the little chest, and we kept the Poore Pasture. We intend to continue as the owners of both in perpetuity. We keep our word."

Ryder pursed his lips. "I need to review my papers. I suggest we continue this meeting at a later date," he said.

"Obviously," said Mrs Dunn, taking off and polishing her little glasses, "obviously the sisters are not making a claim on anything like the whole rental sum."

"Clearly not," Ryder agreed, without looking up.

"This letter establishes that the purchase you believed had taken place had not, in all probability, been transacted. St Winifreda's claim to ownership is, as a result, a stronger one."

"We have by no means accepted that."

"My request to you, and I intend to pursue this with the Master of the College directly, is that Trinity should simply make the convent an offer that is fair and satisfactory. It suits everyone for this matter to be settled as swiftly as possible, I'm sure you agree. Title of a valuable building occupied by a prominent company is in question – never a comfortable situation. It would also be unfortunate if anyone were to interpret the actions of the College as...uncharitable. Very unfortunate indeed. Think of the potential for bad publicity." Here Mrs Dunn glanced in our direction.

Quentin Ryder's eyes followed her glance as it swept over three sisters in black habits, one in a wheelchair.

For a silent moment we read his thoughts: a tabloid front page with our photograph and the headline: College Land Grab Leaves Nuns Destitute.

"We'll talk again. Good morning," Ryder said, and he clicked his manly briefcase closed and strode out.

We were left blinking.

"You did rather well, Hermione," said Mrs Dunn, smiling.

"What happened there?" Rev Mother asked.

"We opened the bidding," said Mrs Dunn. "They sent a lion, but only a cub. And incidentally, I will contact the Master of the College. I don't imagine she'll like the idea of any fancy footwork that would deprive a convent of its dues."

"She?" we all said at once.

Mrs Dunn shrugged. "Yes. It only took them six hundred years. Professor Dorothy Holroyd. We play squash. I'll try to catch her while she's feeling benign. Might even let her win!" She examined her notebook.

"Do you think that somewhere at Trinity there might be a letter proving the sisters did eventually sell?" asked Rev Mother.

"All the evidence suggests that Trinity wanted to buy it for a couple of centuries and your predecessors kept refusing. The college tried hard, but you're clearly a determined lot. Speaking of which, we need to decide how much to ask for. I quoted the total rental income, but we can't claim anything like the whole amount. I'm going to suggest three-hundred thousand pounds in the first year, to include an element that covers the back payment of rent and your legal expenses, and a hundred-and-fifty-thousand pounds a year thereafter. I don't want to push our luck. How does that sound?"

She looked up and saw that we had turned to statues.

"Probably best if you go off and think about it," she added. "By the way, I would like to thank you for the way you've treated my son, Alphonsus. He was a bit lost. Working with you has really helped him. He talks about St Winifreda's a lot. Especially about you, Hermione. I can see why."

Hermione's face lit up like a beacon. She dropped her glasses and a pile of papers and had to scrabble on the floor to collect them.

So Emelda, that was our first experience of the law at work. We were so quiet on the way home that Tim the Taxi asked if we were all right. We said we'd had a shock and he offered us brandy from his flask. One of us took some.

I was home in time to pack the website orders. There are a few jobs I can do from the wheelchair, and this is one. I can hardly keep up some days with the email requests for tiny orange boxes, nunpegs and embroidered bookmarks. Someone put them on a website in Germany and half of Hamburg placed an order! I try to picture nunpegs stylishly displayed on elegant German mantelpieces as I pack them. Rather difficult, that is, actually.

Anyway, the work goes on, and another cheque is on its way to you with this. If you use it for buildings, make sure you own the land first!

Best wishes,
Sister B.

58

THE WOODGATE CENTRE

Dear Emelda,

We have a slow spring here. It's stayed cold for much longer than usual and we had snow over Easter. There are buds everywhere, but still tightly furled. The sky has been like a dirty duvet over the Fens for what seems like weeks on end. Today, however, there are a few tiny breaks. There seems to be something blue up there somewhere.

I have been much cheered in my recovery by the ducks. I have a good view of their run from my window. They are immune to cold weather and give us the daily sport of trying to get to their eggs before the crows spot them. Ducks are carefree layers. They don't bother with houses much, they just lay anywhere they fancy. Last week Hetty laid an egg in a hat Pavel had dropped on one of his visits. (Hermione presented both hat and egg to him and he said, "Thank you, Sister, and thank you kind-hearted Hetty. I am most grateful." This was reported to me so that I could hear how well his English is coming along.)

Last week Rev Mother led a two-day convocation: Our Vows, Our Funding and Our Future. She circulated her theme beforehand:

"My dear sisters, even if this is a miracle, it should not surprise us! We have always believed that anything – anything at all – is possible with prayer and God's will. We may feel amazed that God has chosen to preserve St Winifreda's; a little place, beloved but remote and, in the eyes of most of the World at least, without particular distinction. But apparently He has, so we must simply give thanks and get on with it.

"Our vows of poverty mean we must work quickly. Building repairs come first. We will damp-proof the dormitories and get rid of the rot. We will fix the drains and the roof. We will insulate everywhere. I propose adding a new conference centre: the Woodgate Centre, where we can offer training in rural self-sufficiency and crafts, as well as inviting our religious brothers and sisters. In these ways and many others we will divest ourselves of our new funds as quickly as we sensibly can.

"We're going to be busy! We were busy before. But we must never allow all this activity to divert us from our real purpose. We are not shop keepers, or conference organisers, we are not bed and breakfast proprietors, cooks, gardeners, nurses or teachers, or even leaders. First and foremost we have dedicated our lives to prayer and to contemplation. Whatever else we do, we must never allow ourselves to forget that."

She's right of course. Just as I was getting the hang of running the Shoppe, I realise that the Bishop was probably right: it's not what I should be doing.

I've had a lot of time to think, here in the sick bay.

I enclose a drawing of Hetty, and an embroidered bookmark of my own design. Sorry about the knots! I ironed them as flat as I could, but even so, it suits the larger type of book best. Or you could use it as a tiny wall hanging.

Best wishes,
Sister B.

59

A Completed Sentence

Dear Emelda,

Free at last! Much as I enjoyed studying cloud formations, I'm awfully glad to be mobile again. The plasters are off and I am able to struggle down to the Shoppe and make myself useful, even though they don't really need me and I have to sit down and can only stay for an hour at a time.

I was on a visit when Alphonsus came in last week with Ted. Both had a playful look.

"We have a bit of an announcement, Sister," said Ted.

"Is it a health and safety issue?" I asked, uneasily.

"No!" said Alphonsus. "I have completed my community service order. I have done my one-hundred and eighty hours. My sentence is complete!"

I said, "Well, congratulations! You have done wonderful work here, Alphonsus. How are we going to manage without you?" Hermione and Nesbitt joined in from the kitchen, calling their thanks.

"Our custom," said Ted, "is that the completing community service worker makes everyone concerned a nice cup of tea. So you are invited to the potting shed at four pm."

"We'll be there. I'll bring cake," I promised, and they left to clock up Alphonsus's last few hours.

There was an odd sound from the kitchen and when I looked it was Hermione. She was in floods of tears. Nesbitt was patting her shoulder and handing her a blue catering-sized piece of tissue.

"Hermione! What's the matter?" I asked.

"It's Alphonsus leaving," Nesbitt explained.

"Well, we're all going to miss him," I said. "He's done an awful lot. The website, the planting out in the greenhouse..." Hermione hid her face in the tissue.

"They're...mates. She'll miss him," Nesbitt said.

I said, "Yes, of course..."

Hermione took a deep breath and steadied herself. She blew her nose. "Silly. Silly me. Sorry everyone. It's just I... Well, I'm used to having Alphonsus around. I've enjoyed talking to him...and so on."

I said, "I'm hoping he'll still visit. It won't mean he never comes, surely?"

"Why should he keep visiting? He was carrying out a sentence, that's what kept him here. He needs to get on with his life now, not hang around a convent planting things. He needs to get a job and put all this behind him," Hermione said sadly.

Which, I suppose is true. Even though I can't imagine how we can run the online Shoppe or the website without him, Alphonsus Dunn needs to do other things now.

After Hermione had left, Nesbitt was slightly odd. She kept fidgeting and sighing and re-cleaning the work surfaces. Eventually she said, "Would she get thrown out, if she really liked him? I mean *really* liked him? She couldn't be a nun then, could she?"

"No, you have to choose," I said. "The sisterhood or the love of a partner – you can't have both. Those are the rules we choose to live by."

Nesbitt re-scrubbed the chopping board. "That's hard, though, isn't it?"

"Well, not if you're meant for it, Nesbitt. It's easy and right if it's what you want. It's only hard if you feel you might have made the wrong choice. Then it is hard, yes."

"Is it hard for you, Sister?"

I was wrapping sandwiches. I said, "No. I've been lucky. I've always loved this life. It just feels completely right. Not always easy, but always completely the right way to live."

"Miney and Alph, they like each other a lot, you know. They're both a bit daft. They kind of don't know. I think they're both too brainy and it gets in the way."

"They're sensible people," I said.

"Yeah. Sensible isn't always the best thing, though, is it?" She stopped scrubbing and suddenly said, "Oh, Sister, I hope they get married! It's all wrong if they don't."

"Nesbitt!" I said, "I didn't think you were such a romantic!"

"I'm not soppy," she said, "don't get me wrong. They kind of just make each other better, don't they? More their own selves, if you know what I mean."

And now she points it out, I do know what she means.

"We'll pray on it, Boniface," Rev Mother said, when I invited her to the tea party. "In my experience it is best just to let them sort it out with as little interference as possible. We'll give Hermione whatever support she needs and wait and see."

"Oh, I hope she marries him!" I blurted out.

"Boniface!" said Rev Mother.

"Sorry," I said. "I think I caught the idea from Nesbitt."

"It's quite improper to speculate. It's little more than gossip," said Rev Mother. "Hermione would be a great loss to the order. We mustn't speak of it again."

"No," I said. "Fine. Absolutely."

She made briskly for the door, stepped through it and then stage whispered over her shoulder, "I hope she marries him too!"

We were all perfectly behaved at the tea party. Hermione only came briefly, but she smiled convincingly and you might never have known. Animal and Baz presented Alphonsus with a box of extra-strong teabags because over the time he's worked here they've converted him to proper tea, and Ted gave him his very own hard hat. We gave him a framed picture of a little triangle of land with two cows on it.

We've invited him back whenever he likes, so he hasn't gone forever. Hermione looked a little sad at convocation, but the rest of us were in ridiculously high spirits.

Romance in the air! Well, it is Spring. And it's God's will, if it happens, don't you agree?

Best wishes,
Sister B.

60

THE BISHOP RETURNS

Dear Wanderer,

It is a year to the day since the opening of St Winifreda's Convent Shoppe. I remember so well writing the first of these letters from the empty Shoppe, wondering whether any customers would come, and if they did what we could sell them. My lovely Open/Closed sign is still doing duty – restored after the Bishop's first visit – but most other things have changed. We have a kitchen area, for one thing, and the handmade things in their own display.

Bishop Sheringham was back in the Shoppe yesterday, as a matter of fact. He came for a long meeting with Rev Mother, led the retired sisters in prayer, and then stopped into the Shoppe on his way out.

"Ah, Boniface," he said, looking round the door. "Still doing battle with the world of commerce, I see. I'm led to believe it's going rather well. Dare I come in? No cakes flying about, I hope?" He entered with a little high-pitched laugh.

Nesbitt emerged from the kitchen, and stopped in her tracks.

"You must be…don't tell me…Biscuit…Basket…"

"Nesbitt," she corrected him.

"Oh, forgive me. Rev Mother tells me you are doing splendidly well, splendidly. Are these your handiwork?" he indicated the row of cakes on the top display.

"Yes," she said.

"Right, well, very good. Very good." He turned to me. "And Boniface, Rev Mother informs me that you have an online store that is highly successful in addition to this shop, and the bed and breakfast rooms."

"Yes, they're all beginning to go quite well now, thank you, my Lord," I said.

"Admirable. Most impressive. Very enterprising indeed. A lesson to us all. I do hope you will be sharing your skills and experience at the up-coming conference, Helping the Poor When You're Poor Yourself," he smiled. "Not that you are poor, of course, strictly speaking. Not anymore anyway. Or so I'm told."

"I am running a workshop called Finding a Market for Handmade Goods."

"Ah yes. Like these lovely little…" He looked down at the display table.

"Pipe-cleaner priests?" I suggested.

"Oh, is that what they are? How amusing. People pay for them?"

"In quite large numbers," I told him. "It was a surprise to me too."

"Well, Boniface, we live and learn," he said, finally.

"Yes," I said. "We are taught our limitations."

He looked at me sharply.

"I think that's what I've learnt here," I went on. "I thought it would be easy to run a shop, but it's very, very, difficult to get it right, and the only way is to listen, to humbly listen to what everybody tells you, which is hard. Pride gets in the way. In my case it does, anyway."

His Lordship turned to the door.

"Now that you are completely independent, I hope that you will not give yourselves over entirely to worldly endeavour," he said, with his hand on the door handle. "The life of the spirit is easily overlooked in the maelstrom of daily practicality."

"It is, it certainly is," I agreed.

"Well, Boniface, I must take my leave. I'll say goodbye – and by the way, good luck with your move."

And he left, his sleeve catching the Open/ Closed sign and sending it crashing to the floor behind him.

"Move?" said Nesbitt.

It was the first I'd heard.

We have set up the system now so that the payments for Los Santos goods can be made automatically. They were amazingly particular about the bank account this end – something to do with money laundering (which sounds a good thing, but definitely isn't). Anyway, it's done now, so the school should have a small but steady income.

Emelda, after a year it is customary for the Writing Circle to rotate, so to speak. The next volunteer writer here is Sister Bernard, so this ought rightly to be our last exchange of letters. I could, of course, continue to write from wherever I am sent, but only if you agree. I recall it was the comfort of ordinary St Winifreda's news you yearned for, so let me know.

Your letters have transported us all to your world of extraordinary bravery and adventure. Your life, Emelda, has often seemed to us to be the very opposite of ours, here in the Fens. But when I look back over this year, I find we have a great deal in common. Your panthers and poisonous spiders; our falling towers and rats. All part of the great plan to see whether we measure up to this life we have chosen.

Your letters have been a joy. Good luck, and love to your students and your workers,

Best wishes,
Sister B.

PS Annunziata says the really poisonous frogs are usually brighter and smaller than that one. I certainly hope she's right!

ACKNOWLEDGEMENTS

Besides Chris Bristow, I had tremendous support from Claire McMillan, the best coach in the business; Chris Johnstone, trailer director and comedy adviser; Ken and Margaret Smith, early draft readers; Patricia McBride, writing buddy and ideas factory and especially Susan Davis of the Writers' Workshop. Yasmin Standen and Helen Bryant took a chance on Sister B. and Jennie Rawlings drew a brilliant cover. Thanks!

I welcome feedback from readers: fran@ fransmithwriting.co.uk

A donation is made to the Stroke Association for each copy of this book sold because it started as a series of letters written on commuter trains to cheer Chris up after he had a stroke. Fortunately, he has since recovered. Just maybe Sister B helped him along the way.

Fran Smith
January 2014

5766785R00152

Printed in Great Britain
by Amazon.co.uk, Ltd.,
Marston Gate.